I0529852

THE SEDUCTION
OF MR. YARNSBY

USA Today Bestselling Author
HILDIE MCQUEEN

The Seduction of Mr. Yarnsby

USA Today Bestselling Author
Hildie McQueen

Copyright © Hildie McQueen 2021
Print Edition
ISBN: 978-1-939356-89-5

OTHER HISTORICAL WORKS BY HILDIE MCQUEEN

The Appeal of an Elusive Viscount
The Seduction of Mr. Yarnsby
The Allure of a Reformed Rogue
The Redemption of Lord Barrow

Clan Ross
The Heartless Laird
The Hardened Warrior
The Hellish Highlander
A Flawed Scotsman
A Fearless Rebel
A Fierce Archer

Moriag Series
Beauty and the Highlander
The Lass and the Laird
Lady and the Scot
The Laird's Daughter

Other Books
The Duke's Fiery Bride
The Sea Lyon
The Sea Lord
Highland Archer
Declan's Bride
Ian's Bride
The Lyon's Laird
The Seer

PROLOGUE

Berkhamsted, England – October 1817

THE DREARY SKY and constant drizzle provided a perfect background to the sad state of affairs. Alexander Yarnsby paced the front room of the country estate.

Thankfully, the only people who'd attended his father's burial were close family. The few friends his parents had managed to keep limited their interaction to sending notes of sympathy.

"How is this possible?" Lady Claudia Yarnsby, his mother, repeated while wiping tears from her pale cheeks. "He had another family?"

The appalling revelation had come to light just moments earlier, when a man and woman arrived just as his father was to be lowered to the ground.

"May we see him?" the young woman had asked, her face red and blotchy from crying. Her companion, who looked to be just a bit younger, failed to hold her back as she rushed toward the burial plot.

"He does not deserve your tears," the man had exclaimed to the woman, not seeming to care who overheard.

1

Unsure what had happened but needing to take control, Alexander and William, his close friend, had immediately approached the couple.

"What is the meaning of this?" Alexander demanded.

The woman burst into sobs, her body shaking as she attempted to speak but was unable to due to her grief.

Her companion's gaze met Alexander's, pure hatred emanating. "The earl is our father. We have lived in London our entire lives. Upon seeing the announcement of his death, we came to see if it was true."

Alexander's mother had been promptly overcome by emotion, screaming that they were liars. The entire scene had turned into a shouting match between the woman who'd just arrived and his mother.

The burial was stalled until everyone could calm. Alexander had ushered his family to the house, after the vicar had insisted the family adjourn inside and allow the newcomers a moment alone. If not for his mother's distress, Alexander would have argued against the interlopers being given any kind of heed, but he'd decided it was not the right moment. His time to find out the truth would come as soon as they left.

Now he peered out the window at the pair who remained next to the coffin. He couldn't help but wonder what their scheme was. It had to be money, of course.

"They are nothing but charlatans," Duchess Torrington, whom he referred to as "aunt," said. "To go to such lengths to extort money is outrageous."

Her husband, Duke Torrington, held out the paper he'd been studying. "It all seems legitimate. They have proof, birth records, everything signed by the earl himself."

Unlike everyone else, William Torrington, his childhood friend, remained calm and came to stand next to him to study the couple. "They seem to be genuinely grieving."

"Father had many secrets," Alexander replied. "This is but one of them. So far we've discovered bank accounts at multiple locations. The office he maintained in London is curiously empty of many items, which makes me wonder if those two are responsible for the missing ledgers."

The vicar neared the two outside and spoke to them for a few moments. After looking toward the house, they finally made their way to a hired carriage.

Alexander wondered why, if they were who they claimed to be and had a relationship to his father, did they not have a carriage of their own?

His father's fortune was immense. Much larger than he'd expected. Alexander narrowed his eyes. "Come with me."

Hurrying to catch up with the interlopers as cold rain fell onto his face, Alexander was angry. Now his mother would have to sit in harder rain because of the delay.

William came alongside. "Don't do anything rash."

Upon seeing him, the woman climbed into the carriage, but the young man stood by the open door.

"I assume you are planning to demand inheritance," Alexander asked, not phrasing it as a question.

The male's cold gaze met his. "I will not speak of this at the moment."

Both were extraordinarily unremarkable. Pale hair, dull eyes, and matching slender builds. They seemed to be the type that spent most of their time indoors, rarely enjoying fresh air—or any sunlight, for that matter.

"When will you speak of it?" Alexander asked. "You did not bother to introduce yourselves."

The man's face hardened. "I am Jasper. My sister, Bettina." He motioned to the woman who sat in the carriage and looked on. "You will be hearing from our representative. One way or another, what is fair will happen." Jasper climbed into the carriage and slammed the door shut.

"They've already hired someone," William said. "They are well versed in what to say or, in this case, not say."

"No surname," Alexander said. "Should I assume it's the same as mine?"

"I would not," William replied.

CHAPTER ONE

London, England – December 1817

"HAPPY CHRISTMAS!" THE Humphries family gathered at the doorway of their London home to welcome the visitors.

Giddy with excitement, Vivian Humphries could barely stand still. It was to be a wonderful holiday because her sister Clara was in London spending Christmas day with the family.

Standing in the doorway beside Clara was her husband, the dashing Viscount William Torrington, along with his parents, Duke and Duchess Torrington.

Welcomes and kisses on the cheeks were exchanged as the group entered and were greeted by Vivian, her parents, and her sister Penelope. All together it was a mad jumble, and she loved every second of it.

Just behind the group, the most maddening man stood and was obviously there to visit as well.

Like a brother to William, Mr. Alexander Yarnsby was included in everything. Of course, it shouldn't have surprised Vivian he was there. She took a deep breath, deciding not to allow his appearance to dampen her good spirits.

Forcing her smile to remain, Vivian slid a look to Penelope, her youngest sister. As expected, Penelope had no qualms whatsoever at showing her displeasure at Alexander Yarnsby's appearance, glaring at the man.

"We are pleased that you are joining us today," her mother, ever gracious, told Yarnsby as he bent over her hand, kissing the back of it.

Just as his green eyes met hers, Vivian took a step back. "I do believe Cook calls." She began to turn, but Penelope took advantage of the announcement.

"I will go and see what she needs." Her sister dashed away, taking with her an opportunity for Vivian to ignore the ever-overwhelming Mr. Yarnsby.

"Miss Humphries. It is a pleasure, as always." His deep voice was like a smooth velvet. At least to Vivian it was. He didn't seem to have the same effect on anyone else in her family.

Since her mother looked on, she held up her hand, and he took it. "Mr. Yarnsby."

"Isn't it wonderful we have a houseful at Christmas?" her mother exclaimed to someone. Vivian wasn't sure who, as her attention was riveted to where Mr. Yarnsby's lips lingered on her hand.

"Vivian?" Her mother studied her. "Why don't you and your sisters slip into the parlor?"

Apparently, she'd forgotten to breathe because she gulped in air, alarmed to have lost herself for a moment. Thankfully, Yarnsby was already walking away with the other men to her father's study.

How long had she been standing there like a statue with her hand in the air? It was most mortifying and the reason she disliked being anywhere near the annoying Mr. Yarnsby.

There was a knowing smile playing on the edges of her mother's lips when she looked at her.

"Would you like to see the preparations in the dining room?" her mother asked Duchess Torrington, and they left. Her mother wanted time alone with Her Grace as they'd become fast friends and liked to coordinate the social events they'd attend.

"I would think Mr. Yarnsby would be spending the holiday with his own family," Vivian announced as soon as she entered the sitting room. "I find the man most distracting. He does everything in his power to annoy me."

Clara's expression became pensive. "I do believe that he and William have spent the holidays together since they were very young." There was more to the story, but it was not something Vivian truly cared to speak about. He'd already distracted her enough for the day.

"I truly hope Tommy comes tonight. I wish to discuss becoming engaged." Penelope sighed dramatically. She was enamored with the idea of marrying her childhood friend Thomas Rutherford, who presently worked as an understudy at Parliament.

Clara's eyes widened. "You must not do such a thing," Clara chided. "It is most inappropriate to bring up the subject of marriage with someone who has not declared himself."

"I agree," Vivian added. "A lady should not have to ask a man to declare himself."

"Very well. I am sure he will make his intentions clear soon. It is just that he is very busy." Penelope looked out to the garden and once again sighed.

Vivian took her young sister's hand. "It is not that we do not wish you to be happy. However, we do not wish you ruined by your own actions."

"I find the confines of society utterly suffocating. However, your statements have merit," Penelope agreed with a pout.

To keep from laughing, Vivian bit her lip. The youngest, while a delight, was proving to be as adventurous in nature as Clara. Both of her sisters often disguised themselves by borrowing the maid's clothing to go about town on whatever outlandish adventure called to them.

As much as Vivian agreed with some of the things they did, she'd always been more reserved. The curse of being the eldest and feeling responsible for them, she supposed.

"Ladies," Gerard, the butler, stood at the doorway. "Misters Rutherford and Jameson are here."

Her stomach dipped and her breath caught. "Oh goodness, I'd forgotten that I mentioned Christmas dinner to Mr. Jameson," Vivian said, jumping to her feet. "I must inform Mother."

As she dashed from the room, Penelope's voice was loud. "This will be a most enjoyable Christmas, will it not?"

"Mother?" Vivian entered the kitchen to find only the cook and another cook's maid, along with Mary, her companion, and Molly, Clara's companion, scurrying about.

"Your mother and Duchess Torrington have gone to the sitting room," Molly said, rushing to her. They embraced. "I miss you so, Miss Vivian."

"I miss you as well," Vivian replied, meaning it.

She hurried to her mother's small sitting room to find the two women, each with a cup of tea, at ease with each other's company. "Mother, Mr. Jameson is here, and Tommy has also arrived."

"Oh dear," her mother said, immediately getting to her feet. "I will have to direct that two more place settings be added." She hurried from the room, leaving Vivian with Duchess Torrington.

Theresa Torrington was a striking, youthful woman with hazel almond-shaped eyes and a bright expression. She gave the illusion of being much younger than her true age, a number Vivian did not venture to guess.

"Come sit, Vivian," Duchess Torrington said, motioning to the chair her mother had just vacated. "We have never had the opportunity to get to know each other privately have we?."

"I am pleased that you and your husband came tonight," Vivian said, sitting. "She purposefully left out Mr. Yarnsby's unexpected presence.

The woman smiled brightly. "We were delighted that the invitation was extended. We expected a quiet evening at home with only Alex for company."

"Yes, well, we could not allow it," Vivian said. "We look forward to seeing you and your family whenever you come to London." She looked to the doorway. "When you return to the country, will Mr. Yarnsby go as well?"

With a delighted chuckle, Duchess Torrington patted her hand. "Of course. Is he not lovely? I do hope that you or your younger dear sister catch his eye. I do love Alex and wish for him to be happy."

Why would the arrogant man not be happy? In Vivian's opinion, if the man was alone, it was his own doing.

"I am not sure that he will consider either of us. He seems preoccupied with . . . himself." Vivian stopped speaking at her unfortunate choice of words.

Once again Duchess Torrington laughed as Vivian covered her cheeks in mortification.

"I did not mean to say he is self-absorbed. Oh dear, what I mean is that he seems to prefer his own company." It didn't sound much better; there was nothing to do that would erase her gaffe.

"Do not worry, dear, I will keep this between us." Duchess Torrington became pensive. "Alexander is naturally reserved, which can at times be off-putting. You must believe me when I say that he is the least arrogant person ever. When you get to know him, you will agree."

"I do apologize," Vivian started. "He is part of your family, and the last thing I wish to do is to speak ill. It is the way of the Humphries to have a hard time curtailing our tongues."

"Which is what makes each of you so delightful."

Thankfully, her mother returned and took Duchess Torrington's attention. "Everything is prepared and settled. Let us go to the dining room. I believe the gentlemen are already there."

Upon arriving at the dining room, Clara and Penelope met them at the doorway. The men stood and held out chairs. Vivian wasn't sure where to look. While she wished to greet Mr. Jameson, she hoped to avoid looking at Mr. Yarnsby.

"Miss Vivian," Melvin Jameson said in greeting. His hand on the back of a chair, he motioned for her to sit.

"I am pleased that you accepted my invitation. I did not expect you'd be free," Vivian replied, smiling at him. Melvin Jameson had never lost the plumpness from youth. He had a cherubic face that was not unpleasant to look upon. The slight lift to the corner of his lips gave the impression of being continuously in good spirits. With dark eyes and overly pink lips, he reminded Vivian of youths in Rubenesque paintings. Melvin was the likeable sort that everyone felt at ease around.

A total contradiction to Mr. Yarnsby, who stood on her left side.

Vivian slid a glance past Melvin to Clara, who was having a horrible time keeping from smiling. Narrowing her eyes, Vivian pinned her youngest sister, who sat next to family friend, Tommy, across the table from her.

Penelope gave her an impish smile. "You should sit."

"Yes, of course." Vivian allowed Mr. Jameson to assist and settled between the two men. Of course, it was her sisters' doing, they must have sneaked in and rearranged things. They lived for opportunities like this. It would be the topic of discussion after the meal.

Or perhaps, her mother had done it after all, seating was assigned by her. She'd managed to slip in two additional people without upsetting the decorum that was required.

Her mother sat at the head of the table, Vivian's father at the foot. To his right was Duchess Torrington, on his left Clara. Mr. Yarnsby sat between Clara and Vivian, and to Vivian's left was Mr. Jameson.

At her mother's right, given his elevated status, was the Duke of Torrington. On her mother's left was her new son-in-law, William, Clara's husband. Penelope and Thomas were seated across from Vivian, between William and Duchess Torrington.

With there being five people on Vivian's side of the table, she could scarcely move her arms without touching either of the men.

The clinking of glasses brought everyone's attention to her father, who welcomed the visitors and motioned for the servants to serve the meal.

Once the meal was served, everyone began conversing. Vivian turned away from Mr. Yarnsby to speak to Mr. Jameson, but unfortunately, he had been pulled into a conversation with the duke and her mother.

"Is it not wonderful that Tommy could join us to-night?" Penelope exclaimed, smiling brightly at her companion. Thomas Rutherford gave her and indulgent look, seeming pleased at her attention. He didn't seem in the least enamored, but he looked on her as if appreciating a sister.

"It seems your duties at Parliament have kept you away from us for much too long," Vivian said. "Penelope does miss you horribly."

Her father cleared his throat. "It is important that Tommy become acquainted with the gentlemen of good station there. Do you agree, Mr. Yarnsby?"

"I have little understanding of all the goings on at Parliament. I would imagine that anyone wishing to have a career in politics should apply themselves completely. Things seems to change constantly, depending on moods."

Clara chuckled with delight. "I do wonder at times what drives certain decisions."

Their father gave Clara a pointed look. "The running of our country is a serious matter."

Vivian huffed softly. "Does lawmaking not interest you Mr. Yarnsby?"

"As it affects my businesses and my family's estate, it has to."

"And yet you have no confidence in the system?"

Tommy leaned forward. "If I may ask Mr. Yarnsby, have you attended any sessions to observe? You may find it enlightening."

"I have, in fact, and plan to attend several times in the upcoming weeks. Perhaps I will seek you out?"

"If I may be of any assistance, do not hesitate."

"Tommy is not only a wonderful friend, but quite intelligent as well," Vivian bragged.

Her father nodded, looking to Duchess Torrington. "Tommy has been about our home since wearing short trousers. A very dear friend of the family. I must agree with Vivian; he is indeed most intelligent."

Tommy beamed at the compliments. He was a dear.

"What of you, Miss Vivian, what takes your interests?"

Yarnsby asked, his eyes locked with hers.

"Currently, I have been helping Father in his research of the resocialization of those held prisoner or captured for long periods back into society. It is most fascinating."

"Where would one find these subjects to study? A stroll about the pier or the underbellies of London streets?"

It was hard to tell if he made jest or was serious. Vivian tore her gaze from his and turned to her father. "Father, can you explain to Mr. Yarnsby where subjects for your current study are found?"

Delighted to speak about his current subject, her father embarked on an explanation. Vivian snuck a look to her mother, who continuously scolded them about bringing the subject up.

Thankfully, she was entertained by the duke, so she'd not noticed.

A sharp kick made her look to Penelope, who motioned to Clara.

Her sister had somehow turned the conversation away from captured people to Vivian. "Vivian is an avid birdwatcher and enjoys spending time with a group that splits their time between Hyde Park and excursions to the countryside."

She wanted to gawk at her sister. Hoping to find a new hobby, Vivian had joined a bird-watching group and attended their excursions only twice. The birdwatchers had turned out to be the most boring group of people she'd ever come across. Why was Clara bringing it up?

"Then you must join me and Mr. Yarnsby next week," Duchess Torrington exclaimed with a bright smile. "You will be enthralled at the wonderful assortment of birds often spotted around our estate. We have spied waxwings and fieldfares, and on occasion, even a chiffchaff."

Vivian had no idea what Duchess Torrington had just described; she knew little to nothing about birds. However, there was no way to get out of the invitation. She'd already agreed to go to her sister and William's country home for the winter, and therefore she was now obliged to do whatever it was one did when birding.

"I would be delighted. I am certain it will be enthralling."

Duchess Torrington looked to Yarnsby. Vivian forced her head to turn in his direction. "Alex, did you hear? Miss Vivian is fond of bird-watching."

Something about the way he studied her made Vivian shrink back. "I agree, you must absolutely join Aunt Theresa and myself." Obviously, he considered Duchess Torrington his aunt, despite not being related.

"Ah…yes, well, I will do my best."

Clara yelped when Vivian pinched her. She managed to cover it up with a soft laugh. "I am so thrilled that my sisters will be with me for at least part of the winter."

"I wasn't aware you planned to leave for the season," Mr. Jameson said. He looked perturbed, his brows lifted. "Was I wrong to presume you would be attending the New Year's Gala with me?"

For a moment Vivian was caught off guard by the annoyed tone. Had she agreed to attend the gala? The last time they'd spoken, he'd brought up so many topics, it made her head swim.

"My family has been planning this for several weeks. I will not return until after the New Year, I'm afraid."

With a huff, he shook his head disapprovingly. "We will speak of it later."

"Do not be put out. There will be plenty of festivities after the New Year," Vivian replied, feeling badly that she'd perhaps misled the poor man.

Instead of a reply, he gave a one-shouldered shrug. At the gesture, Penelope rolled her eyes and turned to Tommy. "I wish you were going to the country with me."

Tommy tapped her sister's hand. "My days of leisure are over for now. We have to forge separate lives now, poppet."

Penelope's eyes bulged at the pet name usually reserved for when someone considered another childish or immature. Vivian coughed in an attempt to distract from the interaction.

"I am not a poppet," Penelope exclaimed. "Why did you call me that?"

Used to his youngest daughter's dramatics, their father stood. "If everyone would be so kind as to remove to the parlor now"—he motioned to the doors—"I believe my wife has some entertainment planned."

Once again, Mr. Jameson stood and assisted with her chair. When she turned away, Vivian found herself face-to-face with Mr. Yarnsby. His gaze lowered to her lips, then quickly darted away to Jameson.

After a soft nod, he turned to escort Clara out of the room.

Something was afoot, but Vivian could not put her finger on it. It was useless to try to get Penelope's attention as she walked past on Tommy's arm with her nose in the air. Tommy was apologizing profusely, although it was evident he wasn't sure what he'd done wrong.

"My mother calls me poppet at times," he explained. Penelope glared at him.

"May I have a word?" Mr. Jameson asked while pulling Vivian aside.

She met his gaze. "Very well. Just for a moment. We cannot linger."

When his hand covered hers, Vivian wanted to pull it away. Of course, she'd known the man was interested in courting her, and at first she'd been agreeable to it. But the more she got to know Melvin Jameson, the more Vivian regretted ever accepting his company.

There was something about him that gave her pause. At the same time, there wasn't any cause for her to be reluctant. Melvin was from a good, established family and was well liked in society.

Her father liked him, and even her cousin Todd, who disliked everyone, often met with Melvin at the gentlemen's club.

"I had hoped to invite you to come to my house for supper—along with your parents, of course. I wish to formalize my desire to court—"

"Vivian?" Clara appeared, her gaze moving from her to Mr. Jameson. "Ah, there you are. We cannot possibly commence without you."

With more force than called for, Vivian snatched her hands away from Mr. Jameson and practically ran past Clara into the parlor.

CHAPTER TWO

Lady Yarnsby's townhouse, London

"IT'S BEEN MUCH too long." Lady Yarnsby neared and offered her cheeks for his kisses. "Alexander, dear, you must not stay away so long."

His mother, as always, preferred to remain in London. Woodhall, the family country estate, now sat empty when he was not there.

The parlor in the townhouse had been recently redecorated, as it was totally different than when he'd been there just two months earlier.

"You have been away and did not tell me where," he reminded her.

"Didn't I?" Her lack of consternation, unfortunately, was familiar. "Tell me how your Christmas was."

In truth, he did not blame his mother for keeping the conversation like that of two acquaintances. They'd never been close. No sooner was he able to speak and walk had his mother spirited him away from one boarding school to another.

When he was about ten, the Duke and Duchess Torrington had come to the school to present everyone with gifts. William had introduced him as his best friend, and Duchess Torrington had been shocked to learn he would spend the holidays alone at the school. She'd insisted he come to their estate. From then on, Alexander had spent every holiday with them and eventually, upon leaving boarding school, had moved in with the Torringtons.

Alexander gave his mother an indulgent smile. "I spent the holiday with my aunt and uncle at the Humphries home. Do you know them?"

"The actuary?" His mother nodded. "Yes, I do. The occasions I've been around Sarah Humphries were pleasing. She is a delightful woman. But Alexander"—his mother gave him a pointed look—"I certainly hope you do not plan to court one of her daughters. They are beneath our social stature."

"William married the eldest."

"So I have heard. The Torringtons have never maintained society's standards. The duke shuns his social obligations regularly."

He waited patiently as she continued to tell him of the reasons he should remain in London and take the title his father had left.

"Taking on the lordship will afford you many privileges. I do not understand your hesitance. I must inform you that I find it most irresponsible."

Henrietta, his mother's companion for many years, entered with a tray and poured tea, giving him a knowing look. The woman had infinite patience for his mother and over the years had often been his cohort when he'd needed his mother's attention.

Taking advantage of his mother's distraction from the subject of the title, Alexander stirred his tea. "Mother, I have been meeting for months now, with a number of actuaries about Father's estate. It seems there are several accounts in London banks our family actuary, Mr. Barnes, was not aware of," he said. "It is very puzzling."

"I am not surprised," his mother said, her tone bitter. "Your father had many secrets. Some of which I would rather not know or let them be known."

"You are aware of more than you are telling me. I need to know what you suspect. Otherwise, father's estate transactions and such will take longer to complete."

"Close the accounts. Take the money. I have plenty and do not require more. Just be done with the dreadful business. Even in his death, your father is being difficult."

If Lady Yarnsby was distant, his father was the opposite. Not in a good way. He had constantly berated Alexander, demanding that he broker questionable business transactions. Being that Alexander had the ear of many in high social positions, his father had often demanded he use it to his advantage.

Lord Reginald Yarnsby had been quite wealthy. According to rumors, his fortune had accumulated in criminal fashion. Nonetheless, perhaps out of fear, his father had been a constant presence at many state functions.

"I prefer to get to the bottom of it and ensure restorations are made where they need to be."

His mother sighed dramatically. "Your penchant for honorability could very well be your undoing." She met his gaze, her hazel eyes matching his own. "Tread with care."

When she looked to the doorway, it was his signal that their time together was over.

The steps down to where his hired carriage awaited seemed steeper. It was as if he carried a weighted burden upon his shoulders. Not unusual after visits with his mother, who'd announced that she herself was considering marriage just as he was about to leave.

Lord Winthrop, an elderly man who attended every single social event, always wearing the most outlandish cravats, was the man in question.

Alex sat back into the soft seat of the carriage after directing the driver to take him to an address he'd been given.

Minutes later, he ascended, stepping carefully onto the frozen cobblestoned surface. He looked up and down the street, noting that although there were several shingles hanging from doorways, it was a questionable part of town.

The door he went to did not display a shingle over it. The solid door absorbed the sound of his raps.

"Enter," a masculine voice called.

Behind a desk piled high with paper sat a man he could only describe as odd. Keen eyes framed by round spectacles met his. "Mr. Yarnsby, I presume."

With narrow shoulders, a rather large head, and a squeaky voice, investigator Barnaby Jeffers reminded Alexander of a storybook character. How the man could possibly excel in his line of work was curious.

"I have reviewed your case," Mr. Jeffers began. "It is quite fascinating."

"I was told by a mutual acquaintance that you find out things no one else can," Alex said, looking around the messy space. "I am hopeful."

The man's thin lips curved. "It is true. Someone like me is not looked upon as a threat, so I am often ignored. I use it to my advantage."

"Do you have information already?" Alex asked, his pulse quickening. His father had claimed to be on the brink of something big before dying. Either great or devastating, Alex wasn't sure. Whatever it was had brought on the series of events leading to his death.

"There is a dress shop on Sackville Street, near St. James Square. It is called Belle Monde." The man met his gaze. "The proprietors have been asking questions and doing their own investigation into you and your mother. They have approached a bank, demanding the monies within that were allegedly left to them."

"Who are they?"

Jeffers shook his head. "A brother and sister, Jasper and Bettina d'Arques-Yarnsby. I've not been able to substantiate if that is truly their last name. I require more time, Mr. Yarnsby."

"Of course." Alex considered for a moment what his next step would be. "Perhaps I should pay them a call."

"It would hinder my investigation. I will ask that you look into the bank on this note." He slid a piece of paper across the only clean space on the desktop. "Your father has an account there. The d'Arqueses were able to withdraw some funds, but the banker became suspicious and refused to give them more than the minimal amount."

"If their name is on the account, why would the banker not release more money?"

Jeffers shrugged. "Because they usually presented notes signed by your father. Now with the lord's death, the bank is being cautious."

Unfortunately, he wouldn't be able to visit either the dress shop or the bank until after the holidays, so he directed the coachman to take him to the coffeeshop he and William often frequented.

As per usual, the interior bustled with activity. It was a common meeting place for many Londoners. It was also a place where one could sit and discuss whatever one wished without having to worry about high society's ears.

Outside, street vendors called out to passersby, as many women with baskets on their arms stopped to shop for the offerings. It was London at its nosiest, the stark opposite of his normal country life.

"Alexander," William Torrington called him over to where he sat with Todd Humphries, his wife's cousin.

He greeted the men and settled into a chair.

"How did your meeting go?" William inquired.

"It seems there is another account." He handed the note the inspector had given him to Todd.

Todd, an actuary, had been hired by Alex to help solve the puzzle that was his father's estate. Although a bit younger than both he and William, Todd was astute and already building a reputation for his ability to keep amazingly accurate records.

"Interesting. That makes five," Todd commented. "Your father had amassed quite a fortune."

"Why so many banks?" Alex asked. "And why did he not leave any kind of document that would divulge the information?"

Todd met his gaze for a moment. "What is to say that he did not?"

"When his Last Will and Testament was read, all that was disclosed was the townhouse he left for my mother in London, the estate in the country, where I live, and two bank accounts. A specific amount was left to my mother that will allow her to live out her life comfortably. The rest of the estate and his businesses were left to me. There was no mention whatsoever of the other three bank accounts."

"Or of another family," Todd added.

"It is all very strange," William commented. "There was that bit about you taking over his business."

With a dry chuckle, Alex shook his head. "In an office that consists of a desk and account ledgers, every entry with a code that means nothing to me."

A woman neared and placed a cup of tea with cream in front of him, then quickly walked away. "I'd hoped to order toast," Alexander said, peering down at his tea. "I'm hungry."

"We should go home, then," William said. "I am sure there is plenty of food left from the tea Mother and Clara hosted earlier this afternoon."

They made their way from the coffee shop toward the townhouse. The carriage was forced to a slow pace by the many people out and about.

With all the entertaining, servants were dispatched to every corner of London to find specific items for the evening soirees. From geese to crystal, every item imaginable had to be acquired for London's elite to impress each other.

"I hope we do not have any social events pressing," Alex said to William. "If so, I will not attend."

William laughed. "Unfortunately, it will be impossible for you to be absent."

Straightening, he frowned at his friend. "Why?"

"Because Mother and Clara are entertaining at the townhouse tonight. Not only the Humphries family, but also the Barrows."

"The Barrows?" Alexander had met Lord and Lady Barrow on several occasions. They were an agreeable pair. So much so that their social status had not even been affected by their son's unfortunate fall from grace.

"Any word on their son?"

William shrugged. "It has been almost five years since he left for India. I suspect he will return soon."

"Society has a good memory when it comes to scandal. Even if he waits ten years, Gideon Barrow will always be considered dishonorable." Alex chuckled. "Which is why I like him."

"I do as well," his friend agreed.

"Let me out," Alex said upon spotting something interesting through a bakery window. "I will be along soon." Before William could ask, not that his friend seemed inclined to, Alex exited the coach.

"…and two of those please." The woman leaned over the display case, a basket firmly in her hand. "Add the third one so it won't remain alone."

THE SINGSONG VOICE made the corners of his lips inch up.

"Miss Humphries."

Vivian Humphries started, her wide eyes turning to him. "Mr. Yarnsby, you startled me half to death."

"I apologize." He gave a slight bow.

Her gaze moved from him to the doorway. It was then he noted she was alone. Not acceptable for a woman of her social stature.

"Why are you here?" she asked, a challenge in her voice. "This is not near the Torrington townhouse."

"Nor is it near your home," he replied, then regretted the childish retort.

"My cousin Glenda lives around the corner. I am on my way to visit." Once again, she looked to the doorway. "Are you alone?"

Alex nodded. "Indeed, I am. To answer your question, I am here because I am very hungry."

"I see," she replied, accepting the wrapped pastries from the woman behind the counter.

When he did not move or reply, her cheeks pinkened.

"Good day, Mr. Yarnsby." She rounded him and walked out.

"Sir?" the woman behind the counter asked.

Torn between his stomach's growl and curiosity, Alex decided to follow Vivian. It was most uncommon for a woman to be out alone without escort. A part of him couldn't help but wonder if she was out to meet with the blob of man she'd invited to dinner the night before.

The wind seemed colder as he turned the corner in the direction Vivian had gone. Sure enough, she was alone.

A pair of street urchins rushed to her, and she laughed at something they said. She tore one of the pastries into sections and handed pieces to each child. Together with the dirty children, she went to a doorway, where she entered.

The exterior of the building was nondescript. A red-faced woman lugging a heavy bundle exited and motioned for a man with a cart to come closer. Together she and the man loaded what looked to be clothing onto the cart.

"Pardon," Alex said, nearing. "I am looking for a friend. Are these apartments?"

The woman chuckled without mirth. "Can call 'em that, I suppose." She gave him a once over. "We may all be poor, but we are honest people 'ere."

Obviously, she figured that he was seeking someone for illegal matters.

"I seek to employ a servant," he clarified. "A woman with red hair applied."

"No one with red hair comes 'ere but Miss Vivian. She don't be needin' employment." The woman cackled. "She's a saint who comes to spend time and feed the elderly."

The pair rode off, talking loudly about him. Mostly they'd decided he was not to be trusted. Alex met his own gaze in a dirty window. Perhaps with his hair blown this way and that and the scarf pulled up to his ears, he did seem seedy.

UPON ENTERING THE townhouse, Alexander was immediately directed to get out of the way by William's wife, Clara.

"If you're hungry, go to the kitchen, Alex, but please do not ask for food to be prepared. They are extremely busy for our dinner party tonight." Her eyes shined bright. "My first dinner party. I am so very excited."

He couldn't help but smile at her. With vibrant green eyes and red hair matching her sister's, she was a beauty. However, in his opinion, Vivian was the prettiest of the three sisters, and of a more even temperament.

The three sisters were independent thinkers, which appealed to him. Penelope, the youngest, was the most outspoken, and Clara was the adventurous one. He'd yet to decide what trait was Vivian's strongest.

"I saw your sister Vivian today," he remarked, ignoring Clara's attempt to shoo him away. "She was alone at a bakery not too far from the market near your home."

Clara didn't seem surprised. Obviously, much to their parent's consternation, the sisters often escaped to go out without escort. "Ah yes, she must have gone to visit Mr. and Mrs. Conner. The poor dears. Have no one to look after them. I must remind her we need to hire someone for that task whilst we are away in the country."

"Why does she go in person?" He followed Clara as she hurried to the dining room.

She turned, a frown on her face. "Why would she not?" Her expression changed when her companion, Molly, entered with a floral arrangement. "Oh, how beautiful." She looked back to Alex. "Do not mention seeing her alone to my parents tonight."

CHAPTER THREE

"HE WALKED INTO the bakery. How very strange." Penelope was perched on Vivian's bed, dressed only in her chemise. "Was he as dashing as the other night?" Her sister sighed dramatically. "Mr. Yarnsby is the most handsome man I've ever seen."

"Then perhaps you should strive for a courtship," Vivian replied.

"Ha," Penelope exclaimed. "He only has eyes for you. As a matter of fact, we were all surprised he did not try to intercept between you and that dreadful Mr. Jameson."

"Mr. Jameson is not dreadful." Vivian held up a mauve gown that she planned to wear that night. The high velvet-trimmed neckline was flattering, and the long sleeves would keep her warm.

After running into Yarnsby at the bakery, she'd thought of nothing else. He had indeed looked dashingly handsome. The cold air had brought color to his cheeks, and his windblown hair had made him seem dangerous. There was something about the man that made her lose her train of thought. It was most annoying.

"Why do you not admit to being attracted to him?" Penelope studied her, then looked to the dress. "That gown is ugly. You never wear it once you try it on. I am not sure what the dressmaker was thinking."

"I am not in the least attracted to Mr. Yarnsby. He has been nothing by an annoyance. Why would I wish to be with someone who runs off anyone interested in suiting me but does not declare himself? I believe he is playing a game."

"You should play one back, then," Penelope quipped. Her younger sister's eyes rounded, and a wide smile slowly creeped up until her entire face transformed. "I have an amazingly devilish idea."

"What is it, Pen?" Vivian asked as she pulled a different gown, this time a green one, from the wardrobe.

"What if you seduce Mr. Yarnsby?"

Vivian spun. "Why on earth would I do that?"

Holding her hands out, Penelope made her hesitate. "Pretend to seduce him, string him along, then when he is about to fall, you waltz away. Give him a taste of his own medicine."

"He has never tried to seduce me. Quite the opposite— he acts as some sort of strange protector." She shook her head. "Like today when I went to visit the Connors. He followed me to the building."

"No!" Penelope was enthralled now. "Did he go inside?"

"He did not."

There was a rap on the door, and her lady's maid, Mary, entered. "A note for you, Miss Vivian."

"Is the messenger awaiting a reply?"

"No, miss, the messenger went off."

The note was short and to the point.

"What is it?" Penelope attempted to read over her shoulder.

Vivian huffed. "An apology from Mr. Jameson for being so forward last night at dinner. He informs me that he will not pursue any courtship with me."

"Mr. Yarnsby," they said in unison.

Their mother entered, then she stopped in her tracks and gawked at them. "Why are neither of you dressed? We are about to depart."

They dressed hurriedly, their mother fussing about their lack of care over their appearance the entire time. In the end, Vivian wore the ugly mauve dress. If Mr. Yarnsby was to be there, she wished it to be as unflattering as possible.

Both her mother and Penelope were polite when she asked about her appearance, but it was obvious the color did not suit her in the least.

"That is not the right dress if you plan to seduce him," Penelope whispered once they were ensconced in the coach.

"The last thing I wish to do is that," Vivian hissed. "If anything, I hope to avoid the man."

"What about at the country estate?" Penelope quipped. "You are going birdwatching."

She'd forgotten about it. "I'll make excuses."

THE TOWNHOUSE WAS aglow when their carriage pulled up. It made Vivian's heart happy to attend her sister's first-time hosting. She'd purposefully stayed away that day, even though she wanted so much to help Clara. True to form, always independent, Clara had banned everyone from coming earlier, except their mother, who would have ignored orders anyway.

Now as she and Penelope walked up the stairs behind their parents, pride filled her at spotting Clara standing next to her husband, Viscount William Torrington. The smile on Clara's face was so wide, it made Vivian want to weep.

"Dear sister," Vivian exclaimed once her turn to be greeted came. "I am so very proud of you." She turned to look into the lavishly decorated parlor. "Everything is absolutely perfect."

Clara beamed. "Mother and Duchess Torrington were invaluable." Her eyes rounded. "Oh dear, Lord and Lady Barrow have arrived."

"Don't fret. They are close as family and will be so pleased to see you." Vivian gave her sister a tight hug before turning to greet William.

The viscount leaned over her hand, his dashingly handsome features made even more prominent in the candlelight. "Miss Vivian, so nice to see you."

Vivian found the rest of the guests in the parlor. Duke and Duchess Torrington stood with her parents, the couples surrounding a table where wrapped gifts had been placed.

Penelope had made a beeline to the fireplace and was

petting William's dogs, who seemed to be on their best behavior. The only other time she'd seen the canines had been when they'd stolen sausages and were being chased across Hyde Park by the viscount.

Sensing someone's regard, Vivian purposely ignored it. Instead, she went to stand next to her mother so she could greet the Barrows.

Before the Barrows could approach, Mr. Yarnsby neared, his gaze meeting hers for a long moment.

"Did you enjoy the bread, Miss Vivian?"

Quick as she could, Vivian grabbed his arm and pulled him to where Penelope and the dogs were. If he was surprised, he didn't act like it, his face devoid of expression.

"I know you followed me," she whispered harshly. "Very ill-mannered of you to do so."

"I will admit to being curious, Miss Vivian. Especially at noting you were not escorted."

She looked over his shoulder to where her mother studied her with curiosity. No doubt she'd seen how she'd pulled him away. Thankfully, the Barrows distracted her.

"I was escorted, y-you must have not seen her. My companion Mary goes with me everywhere."

Beneath lowered eyelids, his green gaze studied her face as if searching for the truth. "I see."

"Whatever you wish to imply…" Vivian stopped talking when Penelope tapped her arm. Their mother neared.

"Vivian, that was most unlike you to pull Mr. Yarnsby across the room in such a manner. Whatever is so exciting to bring that about?"

Both Vivian and Penelope were struck silent. Unfortunately, Mr. Yarnsby was not. "Miss Vivian is hoping to cajole from me what is needed for our birdwatching expedition."

Their mother's eyes narrowed. "I don't understand why Duchess Torrington concluded you are interested in birds. I must say, she is looking forward to the three of you going out. Be a dear, Mr. Yarnsby, and go with her to ensure she purchases the necessary items before leaving London."

Vivian wanted to groan out loud. "We leave the day after tomorrow. I am sure Mr. Yarnsby is terribly busy and doesn't have the time to—"

"I would love to take you tomorrow," the annoying man interrupted.

"Wonderful," her mother said, then took her arm. "Come, you must hear the news."

Lady Barrow excitedly informed them that her son, Gideon, was to return from India shortly. It was good news, as Vivian and her sisters had known him since they were children. After a horrible incident—Gideon had caused the ruin of a young woman—he'd been sent away by his parents, hoping to save him from complete social ruin.

Nonetheless, he'd been branded a rogue, unworthy of redemption. With the five years he'd been gone, however, and the young woman in question marrying well, the whispering had waned.

Upon his return, however, the chatter would pick up again, but hopefully it would be less traumatic for Lord and Lady Barrow.

The subject of society's standards made for a lively conversation, much to Clara's delight. The younger people battling with the elders present brought a friendly banter that would end in more laughter than anger.

Finally, they moved to the parlor, where William and Clara presented everyone with gifts. The men were gifted with scarves, and the women with fur-lined gloves. Duke and Duchess Torrington invited everyone for a Twelfth Night celebration at their country estate, and much to their delight, everyone accepted.

Since Vivian and Penelope would already be in the country, they offered to help with preparations.

"I have a gift for you, Vivian," Duchess Torrington said and went to a side table. She placed a box on her lap, and everyone quieted to see what it was.

Why the woman had singled her out was most puzzling. Vivian glanced to her mother, who gave her a pointed look.

"Where are my manners?" Vivian stuttered. "This is much too kind of you. Thank you."

"Open it," Penelope exclaimed, clasping her hands to her chest in excitement.

Inside the box, under delicate tissue, was what looked to be a sketch pad and colored pencils. On the cover of the pad was a beautiful bird with its wings extended. Despite the fact she was not in the least bit interested in birdwatching, Vivian couldn't wait to draw in it.

"Oh my." Vivian's whisper was filled with awe. "It is breathtaking."

Duchess Torrington beamed. "I am so happy you love

it. I find it is best to sketch either while seeing the birds or shortly after to get the best likeness."

Vivian couldn't help but meet Mr. Yarnsby's gaze. He looked on with interest, a slight lift to the corner of his lips.

Even with annoyance at the thought of spending time in the countryside with Alexander Yarnsby, Vivian enjoyed the evening tremendously. Her sister's first event was perfect, and Clara glowed with happiness.

"It is not often I see a smile on your lips when I am around ye, Miss Humphries." Somehow Mr. Yarnsby had neared without her knowledge.

He lowered onto the settee next to her, his crossed legs giving an air of nonchalance he seemed to have perfected.

"I am happy for my sister. This evening is a success," Vivian replied, keeping her gaze to where Penelope played the pianoforte.

He leaned forward just enough to ensure she caught his look of consternation. "And now the smile is gone."

"Should we take a turn about the room?" Vivian stood, and after a moment, his eyebrows lifted, Alexander did the same.

Vivian purposefully walked to the fireplace at other side of the room. Mr. Yarnsby joined her. Since the settee was behind the others' chairs, only her father looked over to where they went, then returned his attention to Penelope.

"You must stop interfering in my personal life," Vivian asserted.

The corners of his lips lifted, just enough to not quite become a smile. "I am not sure what you mean."

It took a lot of self-control not to do something childish like stomp on his perfectly shined boot. "You are well aware what I am referring to. I received a note earlier from Mr. Jameson, stating he will no longer be visiting. What did you do?"

When he looked down his nose at her, Vivian curled her hands into fists. With one look or expression, he managed to make her so angry.

"I happened upon Mr. Jameson at a gentlemen's club. I merely asked his intentions and made it clear that you were not in the least bit interested."

With every word, her eyes went wider and wider. "How dare you?" At a loss for what else to do, Vivian's mouth remained open.

"Deny it," Alexander prodded. "You wished nothing more than to be away from him, the other night at yer home, when he accosted you."

It was true; Mr. Jameson had put her off when declaring himself. Vivian had already begun to plan ways to dissuade him.

"It is not your place to represent me Sir. Do not interfere in matters that pertain to me ever again." Vivian rose to her tiptoes and glared at him. "Do you understand?"

"Vivian?" Her mother tapped her shoulder. "Perhaps you would like to come join us?"

It was then she looked over to find everyone stared at them.

"See what you did?" She motioned to the other side of the room with her right hand.

Thankfully, everyone in the room was either family or like family, so there was no chance of any rumors spreading. Nonetheless, it was mortifying that she had become so distracted as not to notice the music had stopped.

Forcing a smile, she focused on Clara. "Mr. Yarnsby and I have different opinions on women's rights."

It being one of Clara's favorite subjects, her sister immediately came to her rescue. "Alexander, I hope you will come to understand that my sisters and I are like-minded in that we feel women are vastly undervalued in London society."

Mr. Yarnsby slid a look to Vivian. "I am in complete agreement. However, it is also true that without a male champion, it is impossible for a woman to thrive in high society. It is unfortunate but true."

"I agree with Mr. Yarnsby. I give my girls as much freedom as possible, but at times they push the boundaries of polite society. Not to say they are in any way doing something that would ruin them. My wife and daughters have always had a soft heart for the poor and elderly," her wonderful father pointed out.

"Oh goodness," Lady Barrow added. "Since very young, all three have expressed a rather fervent need to learn and study as well. I do say, that is what will make your girls wonderful wives to fortunate husbands."

Vivian hurried to Lady Barrow and kissed her cheek. "And you understand us, which is why we love you so very much."

"Play something for us, Lady Barrow," her mother insisted, giving Vivian a pointed look.

Sit down and do not make any more blunders tonight.

"I KNOW, MOTHER, you do not have to lecture me. It was wrong of me to allow Mr. Yarnsby to annoy me so," Vivian said as they rode back home after a wonderful evening.

Her mother lifted a brow. "It was more than that. Mr. Yarnsby is a member of the family now. You must learn to get along with him. Honestly, Vivian, he is delightful. I do not know why he bothers you so."

"I do," Penelope said. "Vivian has not admitted it yet, but she finds him appealing."

Vivian huffed. "What I find him is maddening. I do have a strong urge to stomp on his feet."

"Well, you will be spending time with him in the country. Do keep your ire in check," her mother insisted.

"Why would anyone wish to stand out in the cold and stare up into trees for birds?" Vivian complained. "If only I had caught Clara alone, I would have choked her."

Her mother giggled. "Duchess Torrington is a delight. I am sure you will enjoy her company. Not to mention that the handsome Mr. Yarnsby will be along. It will give you a chance to get to know him better."

"And yet another thing my family has gotten me into. Why would you suggest that he and I shop together?" Vivian asked her mother. "It only gives him more leave to interfere in my life. Already he has managed to ruin any chance of finding a suitor."

Penelope nudged her. "That is because he wishes to court you himself. I believe this trip to the country will be when he declares himself."

"I certainly hope so," their mother added. "He would be a perfect husband for you, Vivian, being that he's part of William and now Clara's family."

Instead of replying, she sank back into the seat. There was no winning when it came to her mother and sister. Her father pretended to be asleep, although by the twitching of his lips, she knew better.

"Alexander Yarnsby is unkind. I believe he enjoys the game of irritating me much more intriguing than the idea of courtship. I will end up all alone, old and withered, with Mary feeding me boiled mushy food, because of him."

Her mother shuddered. "You paint a horrible picture. I am sure it will not come to that. If Mr. Yarnsby does not make his intentions clear by the end of winter, your father will take matters in hand."

"What?" Her father forgot that he was pretending to asleep and frowned at his wife. "Whatever do you plan for me to do?"

"You will find a suitable young man and ensure he marries Vivian."

Her father stared at Vivian for a long moment. "Vivian is much too pretty not to have a line of suitors around the estate. The reason she has not found a suitor is because the simpletons are intimidated by her beauty."

At his comment, both she and Penelope giggled while their mother shook her head. "Laugh if you must, but I am very serious. Albert, begin to study the men when you go to the gentlemen's club."

The thought of their father bringing home suitors made

Vivian sigh. Every business associate he'd ever brought home for dinner or tea had been a horrible bore. The last one had managed to belittle Clara while attempting to show his interest in her.

She let out a long sigh. It was time to take matters in hand. First, she had to find a way to get rid of Mr. Yarnsby and his attempts to sabotage her chances to find a suitor.

"Penelope, I think your earlier idea has merit," Vivian said peering out into the dark London streets.

Her sister's face brightened. "How exciting."

"What are you two plotting?" their mother asked, her eyes narrowing.

By the time her parents arrived at the country estate to celebrate the New Year, she hoped to be rid of the annoying Mr. Yarnsby.

CHAPTER FOUR

T HE EXTERIOR OF the dress shop was nothing special.
Unlike the neighboring shops, who did brisk holiday
business, it was closed, the interior dark.

During the holiday season was when seamstresses made
most of their money. Of course, if these two expected a
windfall, they probably did not deem it necessary to work.

Through the window he saw several tailor's dummies
and bolts of fabric decoratively displayed. There were tables
with sewing notions on them, as if someone had left in the
middle of making something. He glanced at the etched
glass on the door. *Belle Monde Dressmakers* filled it in
curved artistic letters.

If the two people who'd come to disrupt his father's
funeral were indeed his children, why had he not provided
for them?

So far they'd only approached one bank. Once the
holidays were over and he could go to the bank, would he
find out what proof they had to give them cause?

He leaned back and looked up. Above the shop were
apartments, and he wondered if perhaps the duo lived

there. It would be folly to seek them out, especially without as much information as he needed.

Just then a door opened, and a boy walked out. Hunched against the cold, the boy pulled his hat down over his ears and tugged at a dog on rope. "Hurry," he urged the happy animal, who wagged its tail furiously and hopped up and down with excitement.

The boy released the rope and watched the dog as it searched out the perfect spot to relieve itself.

"May I ask," Alex said, nearing. "What is your dog's name?"

The boy smiled up at him. "Spotty."

"It suits him," Alex replied, studying the black and white dog. "Do you know the people that own this shop? I forgot to pick up a shirt and now it is closed."

The boy nodded, stepped on the rope to keep the excited dog from running off, and looked back to Alex. "Miss Bettina lives upstairs. But she's not home. She went away with her brother for the holiday. I think they went to France."

"Is she kind?"

The boy shrugged. "My mother says she's unpleasant and thinks too highly of herself."

He was glad for children's honesty. "Thank you," Alex said, pulling a coin from his pocket and handing it to the boy, whose eyes rounded at his good luck.

"Thank you, sir."

"IT IS FORTUNATE you were not caught," William said later that day when they met at the same coffee shop. "It could send the investigation backward."

He agreed. "I had to see it for myself. Once I leave London, there isn't much to be done until I return." Alex looked to his friend. "Which reminds me, I will need to use the townhouse."

"You do not have to ask," William replied.

He pushed back from the table. "I am off to see about the fetching Miss Vivian. We will shop for items necessary for birdwatching."

"What exactly is needed? Opera glasses and a warm clothing is what I would think," William replied with a teasing smile. "I must tell you, Duchess Torrington is expecting that you will make your intentions toward Vivian known."

He was afraid of that. "I can't possibly court someone right now."

"You will want to consider making choices about it. If you have no intentions, then you must be clear about it, and stop intimidating anyone that dares to show any interest in her."

With no good rebuttal, Alex nodded and got up. "I will see you at home this evening."

"Yes, I must take Ellington and Farnsworth out to exercise," William said, standing as well. "The mongrels will only behave if properly tired out." William's hounds were named after tutors they'd had as youths. Hearing the names still made Alex smile.

They went out. After dropping William off at the

townhome, Alex directed the coachman to take him to the Humphries home.

The door was opened by an austere butler, whose face softened at recognizing him. "Mr. Yarnsby, you are expected. Miss Vivian and her sister are in the parlor."

"Mr. Yarnsby, how delightful to see you," Mrs. Humphries hurried to him just outside the parlor. "Thank you for taking on this task. I am in the dark about what is needed for such an outing."

Alex himself wasn't quite sure what it was that they were to purchase. They had plenty of spyglasses at the country estate, and other than a warm cloak, he'd not noticed that Duchess Torrington carried anything else.

They entered the parlor, where Vivian and Penelope were. Penelope, always vivacious, walked toward him. "It is the perfect day for an outing. I hope you don't mind that I've invited myself along."

Alex was relieved. "On the contrary, I am glad for it."

"I must buy a new cloak—a warm one since the country is much colder than the city, I am sure," Penelope quipped.

Vivian gave her sister a puzzled look. "You never venture outside. I think the weather is the same whether in the city or out"

The younger sister rolled her eyes. "Of course, I go outdoors. I simply adore walks."

With a soft tsk, Vivian met his gaze. "Mr. Yarnsby, thank you for offering to shop with us."

Had he offered? Alex was sure this was Duchess Torrington's doing. As always, she wanted what she thought was best for him.

Along with Vivian's companion, Mary, they made their way to the Torrington carriage outside. The coachman gave him a puzzled look as he'd told the man he was to pick up only one lady and her companion.

The coachman held the door open and ensured the ladies ascended in without mishap. Alex climbed in last and sat next to Vivian.

Across from them, Penelope sat with Mary, a pretty woman of dark complexion who he guessed to be in her late twenties.

"Where to?" Vivian asked with a daring expression. "Is there a bird-watching shop?" She placed a hand delicately on his forearm. "I do look forward to this expedition. I know it will be most enlightening." When her fingers lingered, he looked down to his arm.

"Yes, erm…" He had to clear his throat as a soft fragrance—jasmine, perhaps—tickled his nose. Had the inside of the carriage always been so narrow?

"There is a shop my aunt suggested. We shall start there."

Her lips curved slowly, exposing a line of perfect teeth. She sighed and finally removed her hand. "Splendid."

Something was afoot. He couldn't quite put his finger on it. He was sure by the end of the excursion, it would be obvious what Miss Vivian was up to.

Despite his lack of plan, the first shop they arrived at proved to be delightful. There were books with sketches of every imaginable bird that populated England. He purchased a rather intriguing guide to where one could find rare species. In addition to paintings of birds, a large collection of feathers filled one wall which kept Alex's attention.

The trio of women remained there for a long time, taking in every single item while he studied the offerings at the counter.

"I am Douglas Clark, and I own this shop," the shopkeeper introduced himself, his gaze on the women the entire time. "I find it quite interesting for so many women to be enamored with ornithology of late. Are you a birder yourself, sir?"

Alex shook his head. "Not as much as I would like. My aunt, however, is an avid birdwatcher and is planning an excursion. The lady in the middle will be joining us."

At hearing their conversation, Vivian walked over to them. "May I ask, sir, what do you suggest I purchase for such expedition?"

The man instantly came to life and stood taller, his narrow chest puffing out. "If you would look at these..." He motioned to the display of spyglasses. "I suggest a small light one for your delicate hands, miss."

By the time they'd emerged, even Penelope had purchased items. The shopkeeper's cheeks were a light pink from all the attention, and Alex wondered how long before the man would stop beaming.

The carriage swayed softly side to side as they traveled on the cobblestone roads to a haberdasher's where the ladies would be able to find sturdy, warm cloaks.

"Are you not enjoying yourself?" Vivian asked once again, leaning close. "I have to admit, meeting Mr. Clark made me excited to bird-watch. He is most passionate about it."

Alex looked across to the other women, but they were discussing the first shop, not paying them much mind.

"I hope you will help me choose the perfect cloak, Mr. Yarnsby."

"Alex, please. And yes of course. It will be cold out."

Her eyelids lowered, and he was almost sure she looked to his lips. "Will you ensure I remain warm?"

Something happened in his mouth, and he choked on his own saliva. It took several coughs before he could breathe normally. "Y-yes, of course."

Very slowly, her gaze lifted to meet his. "Good."

Never before had a single word brought on such a reaction. His body tightened, and to his dismay, his sex reacted in the most unfortunate manner.

The woman had obviously not meant to be seductive, judging by the way she now peered out the window, remarking on the last time she'd visited a shop they drove past. Penelope added an anecdote about her tripping on her way out.

The soft chuckles should have eased his discomfort. Unfortunately, Vivian's throaty sounds caused the opposite reaction.

Alex mentally calculated how long before they arrived, hoping to be in a better way and able to stand without bringing his predicament to the ladies' attention.

"I'll require sturdy boots as well, don't you think, Mr. Yarnsby?" Vivian lifted her foot. Her skirts slipped, and he caught a glimpse of her calf before she lowered it.

He groaned and leaned forward.

"Oh no," Penelope exclaimed. "Are you unwell?"

"No," he replied with too much force. "I am thinking."

The women studied him, so he made a show of pretending to consider what Vivian had asked. If only he could remember what the question was.

Vivian sighed. "Penelope, we should both purchase sturdy boots. If we are to venture about in the country, it is necessary."

"Yes," Alex finally said, letting out a breath. Thinking of ugly, sturdy boots finally helped his arousal diminish.

Upon arriving at the haberdasher's, he allowed the women to walk ahead of him, and he hesitated at the door. The coachman rubbed his hands together and peered at him. "If I may, sir, I will purchase myself a cup of hot wassail to warm up." He pointed to a stand where an older couple stirred a pot over a small coal stove.

"Of course. Get one for me as well." Alex handed the man two coins, glad for the excuse to stay outside in the cooler air.

CHAPTER FIVE

Lark's Song, William Torrington's Country Estate, Berkhamsted, England

VIVIAN ADORED THE drastic change of life in the countryside. Restrictions for how one should go about daily life were so much more relaxed away from London. It also helped that other than the servants, it was only she, Penelope, and her companion Mary at Clara and William's home.

The parlor they were in was rustically decorated, with tartan upholstery on the chairs and deep green floor length curtains framing a pair of tall windows. She and Penelope had just finished playing cards and now sat in front of a cheery fire, reading. While Penelope read a novel, Vivian perused the bird book she'd acquired in London. Despite the vibrant images, her gaze kept moving away to the fire.

Whatever was she going to do about Mr. Yarnsby? It was evident he was very much attracted to her. Despite her attempts at flirting, he'd not reciprocated. It was only because his breathing had become harsher and his eyes had darkened that she'd come to the conclusion he'd been aroused.

"Did you know men's nostrils flare when they find a woman attractive?" Penelope asked, watching her. "Their lips part, and they swallow visibly."

"What exactly are you reading?" Vivian reached for her sister's book and read the cover. *A Courtesan's Guidebook* by Lady Everly Greene.

"Where did you find this?" Vivian's eyes rounded. "Mother will kill you if she sees it."

Nipping the book back, Penelope gave her a bored look. "I found it in our house. It was hidden."

"No," Vivian exclaimed. "I don't believe you."

"I will return it to its proper place when we return, and mother will never suspect it's been borrowed."

It was hard to tell if Penelope was lying. The imp had mastered the best blank look ever, and no matter how hard one challenged her sister, Penelope would not waver.

"Where exactly was it hidden?"

Instead of a reply, Penelope opened to a page and pressed a finger to a paragraph. "Read this."

The words swayed as she did her best to focus and read out loud. "The hardening of a man's sex is quite obvious. A noticeable bulge will form between his legs. One must never…"

"Good afternoon, ladies."

The deep voice made both she and Penelope yelp.

Quick as a lightning, her sister plucked the book from Vivian's hands and pushed it under a pillow.

From where Mr. Yarnsby was, he should not have been able to see what Penelope did after taking the book.

"Mr. Yarnsby, you startled us," Penelope said with a giggle. "We were discussing the perils of finding oneself out in the wilderness alone with a wild beast."

Vivian coughed to keep from laughing, and a most unladylike snort erupting.

His hooded eyes moved from Penelope to Vivian. "I apologize. Did not give thought to the fact that you are not used to life here. As you may have noticed, we have no butler and let ourselves in and out without announcement."

Vivian gave him a droll look. "We are quite aware now."

Instead of continuing on to wherever William was, he hesitated. "Your sister is not at home?"

"Clara has gone to spend the day with Duchess Torrington," Penelope informed him. "We will be going there tonight for supper."

He nodded. "I look forward to seeing you, then." Despite being annoyed at his inopportune appearance, Vivian could not help but notice how his attire made him look ravishing. He wore a dark green overcoat over a tan linen shirt and brown wool pants. On his feet were calf high boots, which told he'd ridden his horse there.

"William is in his study," Vivian said. "Although you probably already know."

"He and I meet daily to discuss our business dealings."

Penelope lifted a brow. "How far is your home from here?"

"Not far, just a couple of hours' drive. The Duke of Torrington's home is almost directly centered between my home and this one. If you recall, it is about an hour's ride to theirs."

"I would love to see it," her sister exclaimed with a smile. "Will you invite us, Mr. Yarnsby?"

The lack of propriety would have shocked most, but Penelope had always been too outspoken and daring. Much to their parents' exasperation. Vivian studied Mr. Yarnsby, waiting for a reply. He looked to her in turn, as if expecting she'd chastise Penelope. Instead, Vivian attempted a bored expression.

"Er... Of course. Perhaps tomorrow afternoon?"

"Delightful." Penelope clapped her hands. "As much as I enjoy the reprieve from London, I do miss having adventures."

"It seems you and your sisters quite enjoy these adventures. I am curious to see what you have planned during your time here." He started to turn but hesitated with a pensive expression. "I do believe I met Lady Greene once."

They both stared with mouths open at his retreating form.

"He overheard us," Penelope hissed. "Do you think he will inform William?"

Her mouth still open, Vivian stared wide-eyed to where Penelope had hidden the book. "You always get me into these situations. Honestly, Penelope, you must get rid of it."

"I can't very well destroy it or burn it. It belongs to Mother."

Covering her face, Vivian peered at the fire through her fingers. "How am I to face him at supper tonight? I was reading the most shocking words."

"Crumpets," Penelope exclaimed.

Vivian gaped at her sister. "What now?"

"I forgot to look to see if he was aroused."

"Penelope!" Vivian exclaimed. "Do not say another word."

TOO SOON, THEY were dressed and waiting to board the carriage that would take them to the Torringtons' estate. The only other time Vivian had been there was for Clara and William's thrown-together wedding.

Vivian had come to William's country estate to spy on him and had ended up injured and unable to leave. Needless to say, their parents had insisted they marry out of fear of the episode reaching gossips' ears in London.

"I am excited to see the house again. It is so grand," Penelope exclaimed, not seeming at all bothered by what had happened earlier.

Vivian looked around. Thankfully, Alexander was nowhere to be seen. He must have ridden ahead.

Escorted by her sister's handsome husband, she and Penelope boarded the carriage and rode the short distance to the Torrington home. To call the grand estate a house would be a great understatement. It boasted beautiful architecture, large columns, and a line of perfectly pruned trees across the front sides.

The house reminded Vivian of other grand homes in London where the most elite people lived.

Once inside, they were immediately greeted by an exuberant Clara, who didn't wait for them to remove their cloaks, pulling them into a grand front room that boasted a huge fireplace and equally imposing windows. There were several gathering areas, and the one they hurried to was next to the fireplace.

"Isn't this grand?" Clara exclaimed, pointing to a greenery arrangement on a side table. "I did it."

Vivian was wordless. Her sister had never tried to do such a thing at home. Her arrangements had always been horrible and either Vivian or their mother had to fix them. This one, however, was passable. It was only a bit lopsided.

"You did this?" Penelope asked with a bright smile. "I am so proud."

"Me as well," Clara said, then looked past them. "I overheard the duke telling Duchess Torrington that they are inviting another family to dinner."

"Who?" both Vivian and Penelope asked at the same time.

"A family by the name of Foster. They have a son who they hope takes a liking to one of you."

Before they could utter another word, Duchess Torrington entered. "You haven't removed your cloaks." She looked at Clara. "I assume you were excited to show them your beautiful arrangement."

"I was," Clara replied with a bright smile. It made Vivian's heart light that her sister had married so well. Not only were the Torringtons an established family, but her husband adored her, and so did his parents.

Vivian untied the bow at her throat. "I cannot believe

she did it. Clara never dared to try at home."

"She did it all by herself. I only offered a suggestion…or two," Duchess Torrington said with a wink.

Moments later, they were joined by Duke Torrington, William, and the ever-present Mr. Yarnsby. This night he was dressed in a more formal manner in hues of green, which made her wonder if it was his favorite color.

She'd chosen an ash-green gown. With her red hair, it was impossible to find many colors that were flattering. Other than shades of green, blue, and ivory, the colors most ladies preferred, such as lavenders and buttery yellows, made her pale skin appear sallow and her red hair look even brighter.

"You are lovely tonight, Miss Humphries," Mr. Yarnsby said by way of greeting. Vivian had not been aware of holding her hand out, but she must have, as it was firmly in his now. Everyone was going to the dining room, and she wondered why they did rather than wait for the others to arrive.

"Where are they going?"

"To look at your sister's other flower arrangement."

Vivian's feet refused to move, and so did her hand, for that matter. "Oh." Her lack of vocabulary was a clear sign she was about to do something stupid or faint.

"Should we join them?" His darkened eyes met hers. His nostrils flared just a bit and to top it off, his lips parted. As much as she wanted to peer down to see if there was a bulge, thankfully they were too close.

"Oh…you're…"

"Are you unwell?" Somehow, he managed to move

closer. She could see the golden specks in his eyes. "Vivian?"

It was only an inch, maybe less. At least, that was what she'd tell herself later. Too close not to, and besides, it was his fault for parting his lips. Whatever the reason, she closed the minute space between them and pressed her lips to his.

Mr. Yarnsby's response was immediate, urgent, and shocking.

One of his arms, perhaps his left, encircled her waist. His other hand cupped the side of her face. And then, his mouth did the most delightful things Vivian had ever experienced. He tilted his head one way and then the other as he ravished her lips. He broke the kiss for a moment, just long enough for her to gasp for air, before trailing his lips from the corner of her mouth to her ear.

"You should not toy with me, Miss Humphries."

The words instantly brought her out of her stupor, and she shoved him back. "I didn't mean to."

His right eyebrow lifted in question. What it was Vivian didn't dare speculate. Turning on her heel, she raced to catch up with the others. What had she done? Now the exasperating man had the upper hand.

There was no doubt in her mind that whatever he'd done, she had to experience again.

Heart pounding, she continued forward blindly until she ran into William's hard chest. "Ah, there you are. I was coming to ensure you were not lost. This house is quite large."

Vivian kept her gaze away from him. "I must admit to

being delayed by all the beautiful things. I simply must return to spend time here with your mother."

"She will be delighted." When she looked at him, William was giving Mr. Yarnsby a questioning look. Not wishing to be near, she hurried toward the sound of voices.

"I WISH TO live here forever," Penelope announced as they prepared for bed. "I love the Torringtons, Clara and William's house, and the quiet."

Vivian laughed. "I doubt you would survive longer than a season. We've only been here three days. I am sure that once the routine rarely changes, you will claim boredom."

"Not as long as I have interesting reading material." Her sister lifted "the seduction book," as she called it.

"Put it back in your trunk and leave it there. You cannot be reading such things. It is not appropriate."

The bed dipped when Penelope plopped down on it. "It is reprehensible that women enter into a marriage ill prepared for relations and fully understanding men."

"It isn't all about seduction," Vivian replied, lying back on her pillow. "Personally, I think friendship is much more important."

"True, which is why I will marry Tommy. He is my dearest friend."

The constant argument of Penelope's that she'd marry Tommy Rutherford always made Vivian giggle. "You are not marrying Tommy. You will fall madly in love with someone else and forget Tommy at meeting the man who will cause your insides to tingle."

"Is that what happened tonight?" Penelope asked, pinning Vivian with a look. "You were flushed when you came into the dining room, and Mr. Yarnsby looked a bit…flustered."

"No." Vivian was not prepared to discuss the kiss. Not until she had an opportunity to analyze what exactly had transpired and why.

As the house quieted, Vivian could not sleep. Her mind raced over and over the kiss. Why had she done it? Curiosity? Or perhaps the darned seduction book. If not for reading about the signs a man was aroused, it never would have happened.

In truth, Vivian was aware that men were sensual creatures, driven by their basic needs. In a discussion she'd attended on different animal species, the lecturer had explained that most male mammals could not control themselves around a female. Humans were mammals and caught in scandalous situations because of basic needs more often than not.

No, she could not blame the kiss on Mr. Yarnsby; she'd been the one to initiate it. Although he'd responded quite ardently. Vivian's pulse quickened, and she took shallow breaths, hoping not to wake Penelope.

It was dreadful that she was in the dark hyperventilating over a kiss.

Most troublesome.

When her fingers pressed against her lips, Vivian's eyes closed of their own volition. He'd held her so tightly, their bodies touching, lips crushing. The way he'd tasted and smelled was just as she'd imagined. Admitting that she'd considered what it would be like to kiss him was not telling much, in her opinion. It was common for a woman to think of a man in such a manner.

The rest of the evening, she'd managed to avoid being alone with him and had been glued to either Penelope or Clara's side.

When the other family had visited, she'd been pleasantly surprised by the couple's son, who'd entertained them with stories of his travels. He was pleasant to look upon and of good stature.

Although, she had to admit to constantly looking to Mr. Yarnsby to gather his reactions. He'd seemed to like the man, and they'd obviously already met before.

Albert, or was it Gilbert? Yes, Gilbert Foster. No, perhaps Richard. Goodness, how could she not remember his name?

"Anthony Foster." Came Penelope's sleepy voice. "Do you wish to speak to me or keep talking to your invisible friends? It is most distracting."

"I'm sorry. I can't sleep."

"You don't say," Penelope replied in a dry tone. "Are you still reeling from whatever happened between you and Mr. Yarnsby?"

Unable to keep from it, she let out a breath. "I kissed him."

"You kissed?" Penelope exclaimed, sitting up and immediately slipping from her bed and over to Vivian's. "Tell me everything."

❧

BREAKFAST, LIKE MOST meals at the country estate, was served on platters, which were set in the center of the table.

William and Clara sat on one side, he on the end and she to his right. Clara wore a thick robe, which swallowed her almost entirely. Only her face and hands were fully visible.

"The room is much too cold in the mornings," she explained.

Vivian had to agree. As nice as the large windows and wonderful view, they made the dining room extra frigid.

"Which is why I'm wearing a thick shawl that I purchased during our shopping trip with Mr. Yarnsby," Penelope explained. "I rather like this room. Eating while enjoying the view is pleasurable."

Vivian nodded. "I agree. It is a beautiful home. Every room is so lovely."

Her sister beamed. "I love it here. I finally understand why you would rather spend your time here than in London," she told William, who smiled at her.

The dogs, who'd been sleeping by the hearth, jumped up and rushed to the door.

"Ah, Alex is here," William said. "He will be staying here until after Twelfth Night."

"Why?" Vivian couldn't keep from asking. "I thought he had his own estate."

"He does," Clara replied. "But he's given the entire staff time off to visit with their families for the holidays and is therefore home alone. He normally lives here through the holidays but went there for a few days to oversee some repairs."

"Is it a large home?" Vivian asked. "I know his late father was quite wealthy."

William nodded. "It is a beautiful home. But massive."

"If I were him, I'd sell it and purchase a smaller home," Penelope remarked. "I wouldn't wish to live alone in a huge building." She shuddered. "I'd be sad."

"Why doesn't he stay at your parents'?" Vivian asked, her eyes flashing from William to the doorway.

William and Clara exchanged looks, and it was her sister who replied. "Alex and William work together. It makes more sense for him to remain here."

"Of course," Vivian replied, feeling silly for questioning them.

Just then, a coachman entered with a trunk and went directly past the doorway to where Vivian assumed Mr. Yarnsby's accommodations were.

From their tour of Clara and William's home, there were six bed chambers. She and Clara had decided to share one out of practicality.

"Good morning." Alexander Yarnsby entered the room. "Ladies. William." The men exchanged nods, and Clara beamed up at him.

"I am so glad you are here, Alexander. We were just discussing your home and sharing thoughts on living in a large estate such as yours."

He settled into the chair next to Penelope, which positioned him directly across from Vivian. His gaze moved to hers and lingered for a beat. "Yes. Well, one of the downfalls is the costs of repairs."

"What exactly needs repair, Mr. Yarnsby?" Vivian asked with what she hoped was a flat look.

The cook's helper hurried in with a fresh pot of hot water. She smiled at Mr. Yarnsby and poured the water into his cup. "Thank you, Rose," he said to the older woman who looked on the brink of pinching his cheek.

"I'll bring you some warm scones, dear."

Vivian was reminded that he and William had grown up together.

"She always did favor you," William teased. "I got cold scones."

Mr. Yarnsby took a sip of his tea and met Vivian's gaze. "To answer your question, there are always things that need repairing. This time it is the ceiling. The exterior roof was fixed during the spring. There was a huge leak, which left staining. It has to be redone now."

"And the floors," William added, waving his hand in a circular motion. "And don't forget the broken windows on the second floor."

Both men chuckled. "That, my friend, was your doing," Mr. Yarnsby replied.

The men explained how they'd been shooting ducks and William had become overzealous and ended up shooting out several windows on the back of Mr. Yarnsby's home.

"What are your plans today?" Penelope asked Clara.

"I wish to decorate cards. I brought paper, notions, and such from London. Join me?"

Vivian gave her sisters a pointed look. "I thought we planned to start our scrapbooks."

"You already have plans today, Miss Vivian," Mr. Yarnsby interjected.

"I do?" Vivian met his gaze and immediately lowered hers to his mouth. Mortified, she quickly looked away.

"We are to go bird-watching with my aunt."

The darned birds. She'd forgotten all about that. The man had her brain all muddled, and now, after the most unfortunate of incidents, she was to spend the afternoon out in the frigid cold with him.

"I can't wait to hear all about it," Penelope said with an impish grin.

CHAPTER SIX

"THAT IS UNEXPECTED," William said, leaning back in his chair. "Do you really think someone broke into your home?"

Alex looked up from the ledgers he studied. "I am sure someone was in my house. I can't prove it, really, but it's a sense I have."

"How do you think someone entered your home undetected?"

He shrugged. "If anyone came while I was away, the staff did not mention it. I am sure they would have."

Anxious for their annual holiday, it could have been possible that his butler had forgotten. But Harold had served the family since before Alex had been born, and in all those years, had not once left details unsaid.

"I believe it happened after the staff left," Alex said. "The question is why."

William looked up from the accounts he'd been studying. "Perhaps because they wish to find information as to where all the accounts are. Studying your father's documents would be an easy way to find out."

A shiver of apprehension traveled down his spine. Whatever the siblings were planning, it could affect him greatly.

Thankfully, upon his father's death, he'd brought most of his father's files and ledgers there to Lark's Song so he and William could study them. He'd not left anything of importance at his house.

"I must find a way to hide as much of my father's money as possible."

His friend gave him a perplexed look. "Why would you do that? You are the only heir. They have no basis for their claim. They do not even have your father's last name."

"They use it, father's last name," Alex replied.

He blew out a breath. "Bedroom doors were open, items moved. Whoever came to my house was taking inventory. They did not take anything that I could tell, however. It was recently, in the last couple of days. It could have been when I was at Haven," he said, referring to William's parents' estate.

He had a bad feeling about the entire situation. The fact that nothing could be done until after the holidays was an annoyance. So far there was nothing in his father's accounting ledgers that alerted him to more than normal business dealings.

"There are regular payments to someone with the initials N.D. Do you know who it refers to?" Williams pushed the ledger toward him. "There, there, and there." He pointed to the entries.

The fifth of every month, a generous amount was logged as a deduction.

Alex flipped open the ledger he'd been studying and found the same for the subsequent months. "Neither of them had a name that started with the letter N. Could it be their mother?"

"I wouldn't read too much into it until you can verify it. For now, let's keep looking and prepare notes for the investigator."

It was only moments later that heightened voices alerted them to a visitor.

William shook his head. "Mother is here. I presume she could not wait until you and Vivian came to her. She is most anxious to spend time with the Humphries ladies."

"I am to spend the afternoon bird-watching. It's an activity I normally enjoy, however, today my mind will be preoccupied with all of this." Alex motioned to the ledgers.

When his friend chuckled, he looked up. "What is so funny?"

"Are you certain that Vivian's presence won't draw your mind away from the ledgers?"

Alex snorted. "I will admit to finding her rather alluring. However, I have pressing matters that require my full attention at the moment. No time for distractions."

"Ah," William said, his gaze moving past him to the doorway. "I must agree. This is a pressing matter. One that should not be allowed to go on for long."

The prickling at the back of his neck made Alex rub it. "As soon as the holidays pass, I am going to the banks and then to see the inspector again."

WHEN HE WALKED into the front parlor, his eyebrows shot up at all of the paraphernalia strewn about the room.

"What is all this?"

His aunt hurried to him and kissed his cheeks. Although it was something she'd always done in greeting to both William and him, in front of Vivian and her sisters, it felt odd.

"Alex, dear, you should know—you took them shopping." The sparkle in Theresa Torrington's eyes told him she found it amusing.

From the looks of it, not only had Vivian purchased the spyglass and book, but also pencils, sketch books, journals, a rather peculiar-looking pair of boots, and what looked to be a walking stick. "I don't remember that," he said, pointing to the cane.

"Most of the items we purchased were delivered later," Penelope replied as Vivian continued studying the items.

If they tried to carry half of the items, birds would be startled and fly away. Alex looked at the items. "All you require is the spyglasses, sturdy shoes, a warm coat, gloves, and perhaps a small notebook for notes."

Duchess Torrington gave a firm nod. "I agree. I used to carry my sketchbook but ended up finding it much too cumbersome."

"I will only take the small notebook and spyglasses, although I'm not sure what I'll be looking at," Vivian said, her cheeks pinkening.

When Alex could finally drag his gaze away, he met his aunt's knowing look. Her lips inched up, and he wanted to roll his eyes. "I will see about gathering my things. Ladies, we will leave promptly."

"Mr. Yarnsby," Penelope started, only to stop when he held a hand up.

"I insist you and your sister call me Alexander, or Alex. Whichever you prefer."

Penelope nodded. "Very well. Alexander. I will not be going, but I do wish to ask when you would be available to give me a tour of your home."

"How about the day after tomorrow? I must spend a day working on some business."

He had to smile at the young woman's happy squeal.

"ARE WE TO ride?" Vivian asked, unsure of where exactly one went to find birds. Just a few moments after leaving the house, and already her nose was cold.

Duchess Torrington wore a dove-gray coat with a hood over her head. They'd insisted Vivian do the same so her red hair would not distract the avifauna, the word she'd learned from the book that referred to birds or fowl.

"No, dear, we are going to walk from here. We have had wonderful luck in spotting many species just a few minutes' walk toward the creek."

They continued onward, Alexander and Duchess Torrington speaking in low tones for the most part. It was interesting to see their rapport, the easy companionship that came from years of sharing a hobby.

According to Clara, Duchess Torrington and Alexander

had always birded together, while she and William played music and discussed literature. She was a wonderful mother who split her time evenly between her son and adopted son.

When Alexander chuckled softly at something Duchess Torrington said, Vivian saw him in a different light.

Unlike William, who was the silent, brooding type, Alexander seemed to have a more casual personality. Although he was quiet and perhaps a bit shy, when with his family, words flowed freely, and he seemed to enjoy telling stories.

Just for a moment, Vivian felt a bit saddened that she was not part of their circle.

"Come," Duchess Torrington whispered, motioning for her to come near. "Look."

Vivian lifted her spyglasses to the branches of a nearby tree but could not see anything past the fogging of the lenses.

"Try these," Alexander said in a hushed tone. He held up his to her face, and she peered through them. At first all she saw was the brown bark of the branches, then tilting her head up a bit, she caught sight of a beautiful bird.

Sunlight reflected off its reddish feathers. The bird sat on a thin branch, its head moving side to side as it studied the surroundings. It was strange to see the small bird so close and it not know that someone observed.

She lowered the glasses and looked to Alexander. Their gazes met for a moment before he lifted the glasses to his face and look up at the tree.

"It is a male brambling," Duchess Torrington said. "The female is just as beautiful, but her feathers are a more delicate color."

Alexander turned to them. "Should we continue on?"

The continued for another hour, the time passing quickly as they took turns telling her stories of the adventures they'd had while birding. It became clear that although both did enjoy spotting a bird here and there, the outing was more about spending time together.

"What is your favorite bird?" Vivian asked the duchess when they'd come to the edge of a creek.

The woman's lips curved, a dimple in her right cheek forming. "I believe the swan. Although I must admit to only seeing them in people's gardens."

"What about the time we saw that hawfinch?" Alexander asked her.

Duchess Torrington's expression turned to one of awe. "That was a beautiful bird. I would have to agree, Alex. My favorite bird is the hawfinch."

Vivian made a mental note to look it up in her book. She turned to Alexander. "And yours?"

"The nightingale," her companions replied together, and the duchess laughed. "He has loved the nightingale since he was a little boy. I think it's the bird's beautiful song that captured Alex's heart."

The wind picked up, and Vivian trembled from the cold. Thankfully, they decided to head back. Duchess Torrington threaded her arm through Vivian's. "I hope we didn't bore you too much, dear."

"Quite the opposite," Vivian replied, meaning it. "I may have found a hobby that I enjoy."

Lark's Song came into view, reminding Vivian of what

Penelope had said the night before. "Do you prefer to live here or in London?"

Duchess Torrington spoke with a light smile. "If given the choice of where to remain, I would always pick Berkhamsted. London, although vibrant and full of activity, is good for short spurts. Here, life is slower, and each day can be savored."

"What do you think, Miss Vivian? Would you be able to live here?" Alexander asked.

She studied his face for a long moment, assessing what he thought, but he did not show any expression. Tilting her head, Vivian considered what exactly she felt at the moment.

If every day were to be like that one, she would not have any qualms in remaining there. Her answer was different.

"I must admit having done more enjoyable things here than I usually do in London. Is it the exception or the rule to keep busy?" She continued. "How often do you eat together, go birding, or do other family activities?" Vivian did her best to keep a critical tone from her voice, but she wasn't sure she had achieved it.

It was Alexander who replied. "I would say we have dinner as a group about three times a week. At least once a week, someone from another estate or London joins us. My aunt and I are sometimes joined by the duke or William for our weekly walks."

"There is more time for such things here," Duchess Torrington said. "We do not have the many social obligations of society. Although we're often invited to things here and there, it is never because of our station, but because of friendship."

The reply surprised her; she'd not expected for there to be such a vibrant existence in the countryside. When her family reposed to their small country home, it was for a month or two of long days, where the most exciting thing they did was go for walks. Admittedly, her mother did go to neighboring homes ever so often for tea.

Upon nearing Lark's Song, Duchess Torrington hurried through the gate. "I look forward to a warm drink."

Alexander placed a hand on Vivian's arm, slowing her, and she looked up at him. "Is there something wrong?"

"You didn't answer the question." It was hard to tell if he jested as his expression was unreadable.

She considered her reply. "If I had to live here, I think it would be enjoyable. My sister is here, and I adore the duchess."

Just as he took a step, she spoke again. "Why do you ask?"

"I am curious. You are hard to read."

The honesty of his reply made her eyebrows lift. "I can say the same about you, Alexander. Perhaps it is that we do not know each other well enough."

His brows lowered. "I am usually very good at assessing people's thoughts."

Vivian studied him for a moment. "I present a challenge, then?" Purposefully ensuring a blank expression, she met his gaze. "Interesting." Deciding it was a fun game, she hurried after Duchess Torrington.

ALEXANDER AND WILLIAM played chess, and Penelope pretended to read while she and Clara discussed the upcoming Twelfth Night celebration at the Torringtons'.

"Mother and Father should be arriving tomorrow," Clara said, peering at the paper where Vivian was writing notes.

"We should invite the Fosters for dinner," Clara remarked and continued. "Mother will adore Mrs. Foster. They have much in common."

Vivian hadn't the opportunity to speak to the woman, and although she seemed pleasant enough, she'd not smiled even once.

"Are you certain? She didn't seem particularly friendly." Vivian slid a look toward Alexander and William. "Are they friends with Anthony Foster?"

Her sister nodded. "They are acquaintances." She let out a breath. "Mrs. Foster is a patron of roses and runs a local group of gardeners. You know how much Mother adores roses."

"That could be something," Vivian reluctantly admitted.

THE CARRIAGE RIDE to Alexander's estate was two hours long. Vivian, Penelope, and Mary were in the carriage. Somehow, probably Penelope's doing, Vivian ended up sitting next to Alexander. She did her best to ensure enough distance so that their legs would not touch.

"High-society members would pay an eyetooth to stay in a beautiful country estate. They can host large gatherings there…" Penelope exclaimed. She'd talked nonstop, listing different ways Alexander could deal with his large home.

The entire time, Alexander listened, patiently not interrupting. "I plan to live in the house permanently," he informed Penelope, who pouted.

Her sister, for some reason, would not give up the idea of Alexander being some sort of host.

"All alone in such a large home. It seems a pity not to share the space," her sister insisted.

Vivian decided to rescue him. "Penelope, those kinds of…ventures are for the unfortunate sorts who cannot afford to keep a property."

"We have arrived." There was a hint of pride in his voice, and upon peering out of the carriage, Vivian understood why. Her breath caught as she gaped at the immense home. The gray house was lovely.

It was hard to tell if it was empty or not. The only hint that someone was about was a cart and horse beside what she assumed was the servants' entrance.

"My goodness," Penelope gasped, looking out. "It's huge."

Vivian smiled.

Within moments, they pulled up to the front door, and the coachman opened the door to allow them out.

They were greeted by an older man dressed as if he'd been doing some manual work. In only a shirt and trousers, he looked flustered as if not expecting company.

"Mr. Alexander, I apologize for my attire," he stuttered.

Alexander waved his concerns away. "Do not worry yourself, Harold. You are on holiday, and therefore I beg that you carry on with whatever it is you are doing and ignore us."

The man's gaze darted to her and Penelope, and he bowed at the waist. Finally, with what looked to be great reluctance, he backed away and hurried off.

"Poor man," Penelope commented. "Who is he?"

"Harold. He and his wife have worked for my family for a very long time," Alexander replied. "Other than His Grace, Harold has been the solidest force in my life."

Upon entering the mansion, a grand foyer once again struck them speechless. Their shoes echoed on the marble floors as they walked to a circular design in the center. On both sides of where they stood, stairways formed a semicircle. The rounded bannisters were a dark-colored stone.

Vivian itched to run up the stairs and begin exploring, however, propriety held her in place. She gazed down the hallway to the left, which seemed to go to a library. To the right, the door was closed.

A woman came from a side corridor. "I am sorry Sir, I wasn't aware you were here."

"Ladies, this is Moira, Harold's wife. She is the estate housekeeper, who should be at home resting."

Moira gave him an endearing look. "I will prepare some tea."

Vivian's companion, Mary, went with her.

"We will start with this floor," Alexander said, looking to the right and then down. "This way." He opened the door and led them through. It was a dim room that looked to be a study of sorts.

The room looked as if it had been uninhabited for many months. It wasn't dusty or dirty, but by the lack of fresh air, no one went in there.

"This was my father's study," Alexander explained and looked to the desk. "I prefer to work in the solarium."

"Better lighting?" Vivian asked as she walked closer to a family portrait. A younger version of Alexander peered outward, a rather amused expression on his face. His father and mother seemed to not be as entertained. "You favor your father," she said. "The same eyes and nose."

Penelope came to stand next to her. "I've seen your mother in London. She attended a social meeting hosted by Lady Barrow."

"Mother enjoys charity events," Alexander stated. "She's always been one to do such things for the needy."

Although many affluent families participated in such endeavors, Vivian couldn't picture Alexander doing it. There was so much she wanted to learn about him, but of course it was curiosity and not interest in the man himself.

Alexander guided them to the room past the foyer. It was a beautiful parlor with a view of gardens to the rear of the property. They meandered through two dining rooms, a small one closer to the parlor and a larger one more suitable for entertaining.

They went up the stairs to where there were a pair of sitting rooms and five bedchambers. Alexander allowed them to wander through the rooms as he stood in landing between the two wings and peered out the windows. When they joined him, he motioned to the opposite side. "There are another three rooms on this side. One is my bedchamber, and there is a sitting room and another smaller bedroom that my parents used as a nursery."

Penelope gasped. "Your nursery? Has it been redecorated?"

"It has been changed to more of a dressing room," he commented with a soft look at her exuberant sister.

"We do not wish to invade your privacy. Thank you for allowing us to visit. It is truly a beautiful home." Vivian gave her sister a pointed look.

As usual, Penelope ignored her and began walking in the direction of Alexander's private space.

"I apologize for my sister's lack of consideration," Vivian said, stretching her neck when Penelope opened the door to what had been Alexander's nursery.

He chuckled and walked after Penelope. "I don't mind. I did invite you."

The room was rather large for a nursery, in Vivian's opinion. She'd never been to the home of someone who boasted so much wealth. When she turned to speak to Alexander, he was closer than Vivian expected, causing them to bump chests.

"Oh," Vivian exclaimed, taking a step back. "I-it is a very large…"

"Do you plan to see Anthony Foster again?"

"Wh-what?" Vivian met his gaze. "I haven't made any plans. Why would you ask?"

Narrowed eyes met hers as if he didn't believe her. "Did he not ask to visit the other night?"

The questioning annoyed her. "You must know that your aunt invited the Fosters to the dinner, and it is she who will be responsible for the guest list of the upcoming festivities." She pressed a finger into his chest. "Don't you dare intimidate him like you have done all my other suitors. I am nearing the end of my season. I wish to marry."

There was a slight flare to his nostrils.

"Don't you dare do that thing with your nose either," Vivian hissed.

He frowned. "What thing?"

Penelope pushed past them and opened the door to Alexander's bedchamber. Just as she took a step, Vivian pulled her back. "We should allow Mr. Yarnsby to not show us this room."

"Very well," Penelope quipped and walked toward the landing. "What a beautiful view."

"I would like to continue this conversation," Alexander said. "Why did you call me mister?" He was about to say something else, but then he seemed to see something in his bedroom. He pulled her forward. "You should go."

Taking her arm, he hurried her to the landing. "Penelope, you and your sister must leave. Upon arriving at Lark's Song, please ask William to come at once."

As he guided them both to the lower floor in such a hurry, Vivian was nervous she might fall.

"Is something wrong?" Vivian asked breathlessly. "I am not sure we should leave you alone."

"Harold is here. I will not be alone. I am not in danger."

Vivian wanted to believe him, but it was evident something or someone was upstairs that he did not wish them to see. "Are you certain?" She looked up to the next floor.

"I promise." He looked at her for only a moment before glancing up the stairs. It was obvious he was anxious for them to leave.

"Penelope, come, we should head back to Lark's Song. You can visit the village with Clara; she has plans to go today."

At the reminder, Penelope nodded. "I do wish to go. I hope it's not too late."

Once Mary came running out and they climbed into the carriage, barely sitting before it lurched forward. The horses urged to a faster speed than customary.

"What happened?" Penelope asked, her wide eyes moving from Vivian to the window.

Vivian peered out to see that Alexander had already disappeared into the house. "I don't know. Whatever it was, I have a feeling it was not good. He visibly paled."

"I noticed," Penelope replied. "I pretended not to." She leaned closer, and whispered "Do you think someone else was there? Perhaps an intruder?"

That someone had hidden in the house was what Vivian feared. Alexander could be fighting for his life. "I wonder the same. We will alert William and perhaps have him return with a constable."

CHAPTER SEVEN

ALEXANDER RACED BACK up the stairs and into his bedroom. Bare feet stuck out from the far side of the bed. Someone was on the floor. Prepared to wake whomever it was, he fortified himself and walked closer. Upon rounding the bed, it was obvious that the person would not put up much of a fight.

The man was dead.

"Harold!" Alexander went in search of the older man. Harold was already hurrying up the stairs.

"What is wrong, Mr. Alexander?" Harold asked moving past him as if to protect him.

"There is a dead man in my bedchamber."

Harold jumped to his feet. "Are you certain?"

"I would not jest about something like this. Was someone staying here recently?"

The older man gave him an incredulous look. "Absolutely not." He stalked around him and Alexander followed. Together they entered the bedroom, and Harold continued until he was standing over the body. "My Lord."

"Do you recognize him?" Alexander asked, coming to

stand next to Harold, who crouched down to get a closer look.

"Yes, I do. He is a local man. I can't put a name to the face right now. You should remember him; he was often in trouble for stealing and such."

"Why is he here? And who killed him?"

"I would have, had I caught him skulking about," Harold replied, holding up a fist. "The audacity of this criminal has no bounds."

"Harold, the man is dead. Your indignation is literally falling on deaf ears." Alexander did his best not to smile. "While I complete a thorough search of the property, please go to the village and fetch the constable."

They went back downstairs, and Harold soon rode off in the direction of the village. On horseback at a gallop, it would take less than an hour for Harold to reach the constable. Alexander calculated that someone would be back in less than three.

Hopefully at about the same time, William would arrive as well.

Since Vivian and Penelope had gone into every room of the house, he was fairly certain no one was about. The only space they'd not gone into was the solarium. Passing through the doorway there, he noted everything was just as he'd left it. The bright sunlit room, with its seating arrangements, desk, and several potted plants, was his favorite. As a child, he had spent many days there with his parents.

Until suddenly, when he was about ten, things had changed.

His father was away in London all the time, and his

mother stopped pretending to care about much. It was then they'd stopped sending for him from boarding school, where he'd met William. Since his parents did not send for Alexander during the holidays, he'd gone to the Torringtons' instead.

After searching the rest of the floor, he went back up the stairs and walked through every other room.

The house *was* ridiculously large, he decided after walking through the sixth bedroom and then to the side of the house where his room was.

No one else was about. Taking advantage of the fact he'd given his staff the holidays off, the drifter had come to the house and made himself at home.

Harold had only recently returned to oversee the repairs to the windows and ceiling. None of these tasks would have taken them to the side of the house where his bedroom was.

He hesitated at the door to the bedroom where the body was. Did whoever killed the man mistakenly think it was him? Would the duo who claimed to be his half-siblings go this far?

It made little sense because upon his death, all his wealth would go to his mother.

Then again, there was the possibility that they'd forged documents. They'd gotten away with withdrawing money from a bank with a document he was certain was not real.

IT SEEMED ONLY a short while later that William burst through the front door, calling out his name. Alex, who'd been in the solarium, walked out to meet him.

"What happened?" William gave him a cursory scan, ensuring he was not hurt. "Vivian is convinced someone is here."

"Someone is here. Dead in my bedchamber. Looks to have been dead for a few days."

William's eyes flashed to the second floor. "Who?"

"According to Harold, a man from the village. A ne'er do well."

"Why would he be here, dead in your bedchamber?"

Alex shook his head. "That is the question I am asking myself."

Together, they went upstairs so William could see for himself. His friend lowered to the floor and peered at the dead man's face. "He was poisoned."

"Are you certain?"

"By the blueish coloring around his lips. Arsenic."

∽

"Is there anyone who wishes you harm?" the constable asked, his eyes darting from Alex to Harold. "How was it possible for Peter to remain here unnoticed?"

"As you can see"—Alex motioned to the empty house—"my staff was given the holidays off. Everyone in the village is aware that I do this every year; some of my staff live there."

"In order to gain access, one would need a key," the constable continued. "Do all your staff have keys?"

"No," Harold replied, looking down his nose at the constable. "Only the housekeeper, who is my wife, and I do. I will add that in all these years, we have never once lost them."

The constable studied the surroundings for a moment, as if expecting clues to jump out from the walls. "To your knowledge, does anyone wish you harm, Mr. Yarnsby?"

"To answer your question," Alex said, "there were two people who came to Father's funeral, claiming to be my half-siblings. They informed me they had hired help to challenge his will."

"Their names?" the constable asked, pencil poised.

"Jasper and Bettina d'Arques."

"They are not here, I am sure," William said. "Probably hired someone to kill Alexander. Whoever it was thought the interloper was he."

The constable glared at William. Clearly, he'd come to the same conclusion but was annoyed that he did not get to state it first. "Mr. Yarnsby, I suggest you do not eat or drink anything kept here."

Harold blanched, and his eyes widened. "Good Lord, I just drank tea and ate cold biscuits."

"You would have been dead by now," the constable said by way of assurance. "There was an open bottle of brandy in the bedroom. I am positive that is what caused Peter's demise."

Two of his staff who'd been called to help came down the stairs with the draped body on a stretcher, carrying past to a waiting cart.

Together with the constable, Alex, William, and Harold walked out to the front of the house to look on as the men handled the body.

The constable neared the cart and spoke to the two in

low tones. The men glanced toward Alex and nodded. They rode around the back of the estate with the body.

"Can you remain hidden for the time being? I will begin to make discreet inquiries in the village in case the people in question have the idea that the killer was successful. I have asked them to temporarily place the wrapped body in your family crypt. Do you trust them not to say anything?" the constable asked, looking to where the men with the body had gone.

"I will ensure it," Harold replied and hurried off after the young men.

"They are good people, have worked in the stables for a few years. They are related to Harold, so I do trust them," Alexander said, wondering what would happen next.

RIDING BACK TO Lark's Song, Alexander pondered the reason for the duo wishing for his demise. If they were truly his father's offspring, he would have ensured they were taken care of in the event of his death. Yet they worked in a dress shop, which he gathered did not bring the kind of affluence his father could have left them in.

He had little doubt that his father had a lover or two in London. Perhaps one had been Jasper and Bettina's mother, however, the fact he'd not left them an inheritance gave him pause as to the authenticity of who they said to be.

What about their mother? Neither had mentioned her, and according to the detective, their mother did not appear to have made any claims. Perhaps she was French and had returned to France many years earlier.

Upon arriving at Lark's Song, they were greeted by alarmed family. Alexander had always known he was cared about, but the fact that the Duke and Duchess Torrington had been summoned was endearing.

He was immediately ushered into the front room. The duchess pulled him into a tight hug, and the duke, normally a quiet man, immediately demanded to know who would wish him harm.

While Clara hurriedly ordered food to be brought, Vivian and her younger sister sat in chairs, both watching on with rapt curiosity.

Within minutes, everyone surrounded a table in the dining room for a simple meal of soup and salty biscuits.

The duke met Alex's gaze. "Whoever tried to do you harm will pay. I will not stand for it."

Alex gave him an assuring look. "I have an idea of who it may be, however, it will be hard to prove. As of this moment, I must remain out of sight."

"If," William interjected, "they believe their plan succeeded, then they may try to gain access to his father's accounts."

Duchess Torrington let out an exasperated breath. "It's those two. The pair who showed up at your father's funeral. Horrible creatures."

As they continued to eat, Duchess Torrington told Vivian and Penelope about Jasper and Bettina.

Vivian met his gaze. "If they are indeed who they claim to be, why would they have to go to extremes?"

"My question exactly," Alex replied.

"Well, this certainly puts a damper on the planned

festivities. Thank goodness we only planned for family for New Year's Eve," Clara said.

His aunt rounded the table to take his face with both hands. She pressed a kiss to first one cheek and then the other. "I am so grateful you were staying here. I cannot imagine life without you."

She began weeping, and he stood and took her into his arms. "The birds would miss us," he quipped, glad when she chuckled.

His voice gruff, the duke came and took his wife in his arms. "Now, now, dear. Alexander and William will outlive us both."

Alex noted that Vivian's eyes misted, and she wiped at one while looking away.

"I will remain here until after the holidays. The day after New Year's, I will return to London. If it was indeed the two, they will not hesitate to proclaim my death and attempt to gain access to father's accounts."

William gave him a pointed look. "I will come with you."

ONCE THEY FINISHED eating, William, the duke, and Alexander went to the study. Alexander poured himself a rather large portion of brandy and took a deep drink.

"We must dispatch a message to your mother, just to ensure they do not try anything," the duke added.

"Yes," he agreed. "I will hire personal guards for her as well."

Lowering into a chair, Alex studied the liquid in his

glass. "Why would they do something so soon? If successful, it would be too obvious it was them who'd try to kill me. Especially if they go to the bank and actuary."

"Greed clouds judgement," William remarked. "I believe after hiring whoever it was that poisoned that man, they immediately returned to London. Or perhaps they hired the person in London."

"When I stopped by the dress shop, a young boy told me they'd gone to France. I wonder if they are near here somewhere instead?" Alexander let out a long breath. "We should all tread with care."

Needing fresh air, Alex excused himself and went out through the kitchens to the back of the house. The normally robust garden was now dormant, most of the plants gone until spring.

Vivian stood with her back to him, a thick fur-lined cape around her shoulders. She peered up at the sky. Seeming to be in deep thought, she'd not heard him walk out. He stilled, enjoying the view of her jawline and neck as she continued to look at the stars.

After a long moment, she looked down, bowing her head as if in prayer. It made it impossible for him to move as he didn't wish to startle her.

He looked on as she kept her head down, and before long, he fell into the same pose. He prayed for not only his own protection, but for those at the house, and his mother as well.

"Alexander?"

Vivian had approached and watched him. "Oh, I'm sorry, I couldn't see clear enough to notice your eyes were closed."

CHAPTER EIGHT

V IVIAN ACHED TO reach out and touch Alexander. For
the first time since meeting him, he seemed approach-
able, vulnerable even. She wasn't sure if he'd been praying
or simply thinking, but when she'd walked closer to him,
she noticed that not only was his head bowed but also his
eyes were closed.

Then the darkened gaze met hers, and she found herself
at a loss for words. What did one say to someone whose life
was in danger? What would have happened had he been
staying at his own home instead of at his dearest friends'?

Although tall, young, and healthy, he would have suc-
cumbed to poison, and his death would have been a
tragedy.

"I came out here to think." He peered up at the sky. "I
see you found the perfect place to stargaze."

"I can leave you alone," Vivian said but didn't move.
"Allow you time to yourself."

"Remain with me," he prompted. "I would very much
like your company."

A shiver of awareness raced down her spine, and Vivian

wondered if it would be possible to keep from kissing him again. The thought was silly, of course. He continued to sabotage any chance of her finding a potential husband while not declaring himself.

This was not the time for such thoughts. Surely the last thing on the man's mind at the moment was kissing.

When he pulled her close, his mouth covering hers, Vivian was abruptly proven wrong.

She clung to his shoulders, enjoying the solid feel of his strong body against hers and the circling of her waist by his arms. Vivian's eyes fluttered closed when his lips trailed kisses from one corner of her mouth to the other.

At the pressing of his tongue at her lips, she allowed her mouth to fall open so he could proceed.

Unable to keep from it, she threaded her fingers through his hair, enjoying the feel of the soft locks as they slipped past. He was a combination of soft and hard, warm and sometimes cold. But in that moment, the only thought she could harness was wanting more than a simple kiss.

His hand slid from her waist to cup her breast, and Vivian gasped at the instant heat trailing from there to her most intimate place.

Lifting to her toes, she pressed against him, needing relief, while at the same time wondering how it was possible for something so simple as a touch to send her reeling.

Alexander circled the very tip of her breast with his thumb, the sensations were indescribable. That he could bring her to feel so much through the fabric of her dress made her dizzy.

Alexander continued to kiss her. The kiss was different

from before, almost savage. She'd no doubt have bruised lips and would be at a loss as to how to explain it. Not even the thought of others knowing what happened made her pull away. Instead, she pressed closer to him.

He released her breast, leaving her breathless and wanting to cry. When his tongue traced circles down the side of her throat, however, relief filled her. His hot breath blew over the damp trail as he moved down her right shoulder, toward the top of her breast.

Vivian's head fell sideways to the left to give him more access as she gripped his shoulders, not wanting him to move away.

Then he reached her right breast. This time his hand dipped into her bodice to free it. To her delight he took the pink tip into his mouth, Vivian had to bite her bottom lip to keep from crying out as the most exquisite of sensations overcame her.

"Oh," she gasped when he pulled the nipple into his mouth, suckling on it and sending rivulets of heat to pool at her very core. "Oh," Vivian repeated as her head fell back.

He'd have to stop soon, she considered. Someone could walk out and see…

All thoughts vanished as something strange happened. Her entire body stiffened, the heat pooling to the point that it was as if it would explode.

Once again, he kissed his way back to her mouth. His hand took her breast, and he pinched the tip of it just as his tongue drove past her lips.

Vivian swooned, her body becoming limp, then something marvelous happened that she'd never be able to explain. It was as if all the stars above them moved in circles.

Her fingers dug into his coat as she feared falling. "We must stop," she finally managed to say.

Alexander pulled her against him, his breathing as labored as hers, and she wondered if his heart hammered as hard as hers did.

"You should release me," she finally managed. "It is not proper." The words were silly, of course, but what else could she do? Now that she'd allowed the man much too many liberties, there was nothing to be said that could repair it. That he'd still not declared his intentions made her angry at herself.

"You are the most beautiful woman I have ever kissed," Alexander said, pressing a light kiss to her lips. "I wish we could continue forever."

The comment, although meant as a compliment, annoyed her, and she pushed him away. At the cold air hitting her breast, she gasped and arranged the bodice, her cheeks burning. "This will not happen again."

She went to round him, but he blocked her way. "You should wait a moment and allow the flushing of your face to cool."

"Crumpets," she muttered, knowing he was right. She walked a few feet away from him, keeping her back to the irritating man.

"Why do you do what you do? Turn men away who attempt to court me?" Vivian asked. "If you do not wish to marry me, it would be best if you stayed away from me."

He didn't reply, which made her angry.

"I mean it. I do not wish for you to even speak to me again."

When he didn't reply, she blew out a breath. "You are very, very annoying."

"I am?" Penelope asked. "Why? What did I do?"

Vivian turned around to find only her sister standing there.

"I was speaking to Alexander," Vivian said, shaking her head. "He is quite irritating."

"Oh," Penelope said, biting her bottom lip. "What exactly happened? It seems to have angered the duke."

As much as she wanted to, Vivian did her best to keep her voice even. "Why would the duke care about a conversation between Alexander and me?"

"Because the duke just told Alexander they had to talk." Penelope gave her a worried look. "He said he'd seen what happened out here."

Vivian's stomach plummeted, and her face burned hot. "Oh no." She covered her face with both hands and sunk to the closest bench. "Oh no."

"It's very cold out here. We should go inside."

"No. No. No." Vivian shook her head. "How will I ever face any of them?"

Penelope looked over her shoulder. "I am sure the duke's catching you and Alexander arguing is nothing to be ashamed of."

"We were not arguing," Vivian exclaimed, her head falling back. "We were kissing…more than just kissing…my breast… Oh God." Vivian stood and raced blindly through the house and up the stairs to her room.

IT WAS ONLY seconds later that Duchess Torrington, Clara, Penelope, and even Mary all rushed into the room. Vivian was surrounded as she covered her face, repeating, "Oh my God," over and over. It was unclear if she was on the brink of crying or laughing hysterically as both reactions threatened.

"The duke caught her and Mr. Yarnsby in the most embarrassing state," Penelope explained, which made Vivian let out a groan.

Clara lowered so she could look her in the face. Vivian knew this because she peered through her fingers. "Vivian, what exactly were you two doing?"

"They were having a passionate escapade," Penelope answered for her. "I believe Vivian's breast was out."

"Penelope!" someone said.

Duchess Torrington let out a bark of laughter, which made Vivian drop her hands and gape at her.

Then Clara began to giggle. "The poor duke…" Her sister couldn't finish as she continued to laugh. "No wonder he was so flushed."

"This is not in the least bit funny," Vivian said, annoyed they could find humor in her most embarrassing moment. "I can never face the duke again. Or Mr. Yarnsby, for that matter."

The duchess lowered into a chair next to hers. "It isn't something we have not seen before. We raised two hot-blooded boys, after all. Right now, my husband is lecturing Alex and demanding he declare his intentions."

Vivian's eyes widened. "I don't want him forced to do something he doesn't wish. Besides, shouldn't we be focusing on the fact someone tried to kill him?"

"This is a welcome distraction," Duchess Torrington said with a warm smile. "That other bothersome business will be taken care of soon enough. For now, I do believe we should wait and see about what Alex does next. I, for one, am exhausted and seeking my bed. I think we should all wait until morning." She patted Vivian's hand. "Don't be embarrassed. I expect to see you at breakfast." Duchess Torrington stood, and after Clara hugged Vivian, they left.

Penelope lay on her stomach and studied Vivian. "He must be the one you're meant to marry. Alexander Yarnsby brought you away from your inhibitions. How interesting."

"I do not wish to speak about it anymore."

"Ah, but it's true," Penelope continued, undeterred. "Of the three of us, you are the one who's always in control, rarely does anything rash, and thinks things into the ground before doing them. Do you not find it hard to believe that something like this happened to you and not me? If Tommy kissed me like Mr. Yarnsby kisses you, I would have been in complete disarray, probably half undressed when the duke happened upon us."

Despite the situation, Vivian giggled. "You paint the most vivid of pictures, dear sister."

"You see, then?" Penelope continued. "When he proposes tomorrow, you must say yes."

"What?" Vivian, was bent over and removing her dress,

lost her balance and fell onto the floor, her legs tangled in the skirts. "Ouch."

"Marriage," Penelope said as she hurried over to help her up. "I am sure the duke is insisting he marry you. How else do you think this entire situation will be dealt with?"

Halfway up, her feet still in the skirts, Vivian gave up and sank down on the floor. "I don't know. If it was you this happened to, or even Clara…"

"You would tell us that we would have to expect the repercussions of our actions."

She was right, of course, but Vivian wasn't about to accept it. Instead, she looked to the door, discarding one idea after the other. Running away wouldn't work since the carriages and horses belonged to William. Speaking to Alexander wouldn't work. With her luck, the duke would catch her sneaking into his room. She looked to the window and considered if she could make it to her aunt and uncle's estate that wasn't too far. On horseback, half a day, on foot…

"What is so horrible about marrying him?" Penelope asked. "He is wealthy, of good social standing, soft spoken, and extraordinarily handsome."

"I suppose that is the one thing holding me back. He could marry anyone of any social standing. If he accepted his father's title, he would be a lord. I am but a commoner with no desire of wealth or social standing. Why would he want to marry me?"

Penelope gave her a droll look. "Because you're beautiful. Mr. Yarnsby has had his eye on you since the first day."

"I wish for a home where my husband and I can live in

peace and raise our children without the burden of society watching everything we do." Vivian sighed. In truth, she pictured him when thinking of a husband and children.

"Sounds like a life at his estate. Far from society, yet you can travel to London whenever you wish. You'd not only have Clara near, but also our aunt and uncle." Penelope pouted. "I just considered that with both of you here, I would remain all alone with only Glenda for company on occasion."

"We should sleep. Perhaps this is all for naught, and the duke and Alexander will pretend nothing occurred."

Vivian stared up at the ceiling, the darkness of the room giving her comfort. She dreaded having to face everyone at the breakfast table. This was a situation she'd never thought to find herself in.

Suddenly, she sat up, her eyes wide.

Her parents were to arrive the next day.

Duchess Torrington would feel it her obligation to inform her mother of what had occurred, and surely the duke would speak to her father.

"Ugh," Vivian exclaimed, falling back onto her pillow.

CHAPTER NINE

A S THE MORNING sun trickled past the curtains, playing lightly upon his bedding and floor, Alexander considered what the day would bring. He didn't budge from under the warmth of the covers, enjoying the silence of the early morning.

He'd been up late with his uncle and William. The duke was clear that he was to marry Vivian Humphries. William had tried to dissuade his father, stating it was a moment of passion that would not affect Vivian negatively since no one was witness to what had occurred. In the end, the duke had put his foot down.

The man who was like a father to him had looked him in the eye. "Tell me you do not care for Vivian Humphries, and I will ensure she finds a husband."

He'd been struck silent. "What do you mean?"

"I will find her a husband quickly, perhaps Anthony Foster," the duke stated.

"That fop?" Alexander huffed.

"Do you care for her?" He continued the unblinking eye contact.

Finally, he'd looked way. "I do."

"Very well, then, the matter is settled."

William had poured three glasses of brandy and insisted they toast to his happiness.

In a way, it was as if a burden was lifted from his shoulders. It was what he'd always wanted. A family like the Torringtons with demonstrations of love aplenty. Valuable time spent together and always knowing they would stand with him. Vivian was already basically a member of the family, and she was well-liked by the Torringtons.

Alex blew out a breath. The following week, he'd go to London to find out what the pair of interlopers were up to. They would no doubt be showing up at the estate manager's office first thing with forged certificates of his untimely demise and some sort of Will and Testament.

Thankfully, his mother was under guard. Probably in a sour mood as he'd demanded she remain at home and not attend whatever myriad social affairs she'd been invited to.

She'd promptly sent a note, blaming him for tempting someone to murder him.

Some women did not have maternal instincts. His mother was not a bad or unkind person. She was someone who considered him more of an acquaintance than a son. Often when they'd spent time together, it was as if she wished to be elsewhere. No doubt he reminded her of the husband who had betrayed her. Then again, her marriage had never been a happy one. Theirs had been an arranged marriage, forced upon two young, incompatible people by their parents for social gain.

When there was a rap at the door, he called for whoever

it was to enter. He sat up, then fell back upon seeing the duke enter.

"I want to ensure you will be at breakfast. I have decided that you will wait until her parents arrive to declare your intentions. Until then, I will assure Vivian and her sisters all is well."

"Do you think they are unassured?"

At fifty, Reginald Torrington has been married to the love of his life for just over thirty years. They'd married quite young, he on the crest of twenty and she at seventeen. Both remained handsome and youthful. Alex had often caught sight of them exchanging secret looks or lingering touches. Each time, he'd found it warmed his heart to know they loved each other so much.

When young lads, he and William had often teased them. They'd replied with, "One day you will find someone you will love and won't care if you are teased about it."

"Did you hear me?" the duke asked with a frown.

"I will do as you wish. However, I would like to speak to her in private."

"With a chaperone, of course."

"Uncle…"

"Your aunt or Clara, you decide."

"My aunt," he finally replied, doing his best not to roll his eyes at the idea. It wasn't as if he were a boy who could not control himself.

"Now," the duke said, "be sure to look your best. Her parents will be arriving late morning."

"Did you and Aunt Theresa spend the night here?"

"Of course," the duke replied. "We had to be here this morning."

With a final nod as if proud of himself, the duke walked out.

"Chaperone. Look my best," Alex mumbled as he slipped from the bed. Instead of dressing, he put his robe on and stared out the window. "This is an informal house," he said to the view. "Why should I worry about how to dress?"

He was acting like a spoiled lad. At that realization, Alex's reflection showed his eyes widening. Spinning around, he went to search out his clothes for the day.

∽

"DID YOU SLEEP well, darling?" his aunt called out as he entered the dining room. Everyone was there at the table. Every pair of eyes but Vivian's was directed at him.

"Very well, thank you, Aunt Theresa," he said, nearing and placing a kiss on her cheek. "And you?"

Her eyes danced with mirth. "I couldn't sleep a wink. Too excited about everything."

Everything.

Alexander lowered to the empty seat across from Vivian. She pushed her food from one side of the plate to the other, refusing to make eye contact. "I suppose everyone is waiting to hear what I have to say about last night's occurrence," he started.

"Alexander," the duke warned. "We can discuss it later."

"I think it's best you tell us what you have to say," Clara said with a warm look.

Vivian lifted her gaze and looked to him with curiosity. Her right brow rose in question.

"Vivian, upon your parents' arrival, I will ask for your hand in marriage. Not because I am forced to, but because you are right. I have sabotaged every man who has tried to court you. I did it because I've always wished to court you myself. However, I wished to wait until all the mess with my father's estate was over."

"And that no one is trying to kill you," Penelope, ever helpful, added.

"Since you've decided to speak now, may I remind you of what else you should do?" the duke prodded.

"Reginald, let him eat," his aunt said, patting his hand. "He needs some sustenance."

"Miss Vivian, I owe you an apology for my lack of control over my passions," Alex said.

His aunt gasped, Clara and Vivian gawked, and Penelope laughed.

His uncle began to cough after choking on whatever he was drinking, which prodded William to hit him on the back rather hard.

"I will say," Clara said. "We are certainly an entertaining family."

ONCE BREAKFAST WAS over, Alexander asked Vivian to

speak in private. At this point, his uncle had given up waiting and gone for a walk, claiming to be in dire need of fresh air and nature. Clara and Penelope also disappeared, and William was promptly ensconced in his study.

His aunt was somewhere in the house, but Alexander couldn't find her.

They walked into a small sitting room that had a view of the meadow and corrals where the horses were kept. Vivian went to the window and peered out. "Did you mean to apologize or to shock?"

"Apologize," he insisted. "Although, arguably, my choice of words should have been different."

She turned to look at him. Vivian was always beautiful but dressed in pale blue with her hair pulled into a simple style, she was breathtaking. Everything about her from her pouty lips to the slight lift of her nose called to him.

"Yes. Although memorable, I would not call it a proper apology." There was a buttery hoarseness to her voice that seemed to reach out and caress his face. "I accept it, although I must admit that I too lost control of my senses."

"How do you feel about us marrying?" His heart thudded at uttering the question, and he took a breath. "I know it's not quite planned."

Visibly swallowing, she seemed to search for what to say. "This may sound unbecoming, but I am pressed to find the words to say it any other way." She hesitated. "As much as I've tried to fight my feelings, I am quite enamored of you, Alexander Yarnsby."

Vivian continued, "That is to say…" Her lips twitched, but she managed a smile. "I am not averse to the idea of marriage."

"I am glad to hear it." He replied and took a step forward, only to stop when his aunt entered the room.

Theresa Torrington beamed. "I remained outside the doorway, even though your uncle insisted I enter. I am so pleased," his aunt exclaimed, wiping a tear and rushing to him. "I love you so, Alex, and wish you to be happy."

Vivian sniffed, and his aunt hurried to her. When he moved closer, Duchess Torrington held out an arm. "Go see William. I believe he has a plan for when you go to London next week."

WILLIAM LOOKED UP when he entered, then returned his attention to his ledgers. Alex sat at his own separate desk, listening to the scratching of William's quill over the paper.

The writing on the documents before him went in and out of focus. He could not concentrate long enough to read an entire sentence. In truth, his mind was split between wishing to be alone with Vivian and going to London and ensuring his father's money was not stolen.

"The ledger from your father's office in London listed household expenditures and the bank account your father had here locally, correct?" William asked.

"Yes," Alex replied. "I have since informed the local banker of what occurred." He straightened. "I should go see if anyone has contacted him."

William pushed away from his desk and stood. "Exactly what I was thinking, which is why I had two horses prepared for us."

"The bank is not open today. It is New Year's Eve."

"I am sure Mr. Brown will not mind us stopping by his home for just a moment to inform him of the situation."

Alex considered it. "If they spoke to him lately, it may be evidence against them." They walked out. "I will go fetch my coat while you inform Clara and Aunt Theresa. I would like to make inquiries about the dead man while we are there."

Although it was a cold day, being out on horseback made up for it. Alex and William rode at a steady pace to the nearby village to ensure they return before the afternoon.

"I cannot understand why anyone would wish to live in London," William said as he looked around. "It is hard to breathe past the stench of the city."

"Although vibrant and filled with activity, I agree with you. It takes days to adjust to the smell."

The village came into view, and they rode directly to the banker's house. Mr. Brown seemed glad for company and invited them inside for a cup of hot tea. After explaining what had happened, he informed them that no one had stopped by to see him.

Next, they went to find the constable and were surprised to find him in his office.

He met them at the door with a bright smile. "I'd hoped to see you, Mr. Yarnsby."

"Didn't expect for you to be working," Alex replied.

The man shrugged. "Not much for us to do except continue work as usual. We are not privy to exclusive social gatherings and such." The man's demeanor changed as he leaned closer. "I got a wife and five daughters at the house. Enough noise to make a man mad."

"Did anyone come to see about the dead man?" William asked. "Family?"

The constable shook his head. "No, he was always by himself. Never knew where he came from. He wouldn't say. Yours is not the first house he's made himself welcome to." The constable waited a bit. "I planned to come out to inform you of other things I've uncovered."

They also learned it was certain the dead man had been poisoned, and the brandy in the decanter was the cause.

As they rode back to Lark's Song, Alexander considered what lay ahead. He'd have to speak to Vivian's father, whom he'd met before. Albert Humphries was an amicable man, an actuary to some of the most prestigious families in London. A quiet man who preferred his overly cluttered study to social events. Alex found he liked the man.

In all honesty, he was glad to be marrying Vivian for more than the obvious attraction between them. The Humphries family and the Torringtons got along marvelously, which would make his marriage an easy transition for everyone involved.

"Do you realize we are marrying sisters?" he asked William.

"Why would that be odd?" William responded. "We grew up together. It only makes sense that we are attracted to women who were raised by the same parents."

"They are very different, however," Alex said. "Clara is outgoing and vivacious, while Vivian is more reserved."

"Do not make the mistake to think it makes her demure. She is a Humphries, after all."

Alex chuckled. "I am well aware."

When Lark's Song came into view, the Humphries carriage was already there. Alex wondered what had happened inside. His aunt and uncle had probably already informed them of the new development.

"It may prove lucky that Mr. Humphries is here," Alex remarked. "I may ask that he review the ledger with all the codes. Perhaps he will be able to decipher where my father was spending money."

"That is a grand idea," William said. "My eyes hurt from staring at them for all these days. I do not see how anyone would purposely want to do it for a living."

"In that we agree," Alex replied. "Now I must face my future parents-in-law and get the business of declaring my intentions over and done with."

Although he was a bit nervous, in truth, he was glad for what was about to happen. The only missing piece was that his mother was not there.

"Did you notice there are two carriages?" William said, pointing to a second carriage near the stables. "Your mother is here."

CHAPTER TEN

L ADY CLAUDIA YARNSBY was not what Vivian had
expected. Although older than her mother, she seemed
younger, not so much in looks, but in the way she acted.
Upon entering, she'd greeted everyone, then began
bemoaning the social events she was missing. Instead of
being concerned for Alexander's welfare, she blamed him
for ruining her holiday season.

"There are to be four balls just this week," she told
Vivian, who remained in the sitting room with her.
Everyone else had made excuses and left. She'd not been so
lucky, as just before walking out, Duchess Torrington had
asked that she remain as tea was being brought. The
duchess had then grabbed her mother's hand and escaped.

"The good thing is that the upcoming spring season
will be wonderful," Vivian said, not giving much care about
it. As much as she enjoyed attending occasional affairs, her
mother thankfully allowed them to they pick and choose
which ones they went to.

Lady Yarnsby gave her a droll look. "I must speak to
Alexander and see that he takes care of this threat nonsense

immediately." She looked to the doorway. "Should he not be back by now?"

"Yes, any moment," Vivian said, praying it was true. It was taking all her willpower not to say something she'd regret.

"I am pleased he plans to marry." Lady Yarnsby studied her. "Please convince him to take his title. Although I already address him as Lord Yarnsby when speaking of him in social circles. Everyone is aware he does not use it. Most irrational."

"Are you aware that a man is dead because whoever poisoned the brandy thought it was him?"

"Of course, most dreadful situation. I am sure it was someone here whom Alexander has some sort of quarrel with. It should not impact my life in London."

Vivian stood, unable to keep her tongue in check any longer. "He is your son. His life is in jeopardy, and all you can think about is your social agenda? I fear that I cannot remain in the room with you right now, madam." She turned to walk out to see that Alexander stood in the doorway.

"I am glad you are to marry someone who truly cares for you, Alexander," Lady Yarnsby said, not at all bothered by her outburst. "As for me, I have decided not to marry. I find that widowhood suits me much better."

"If that is what you prefer, Mother." Alexander met Vivian's gaze. "Please stay."

With measured movements, Alexander went to his mother and kissed her cheeks. He sat on the settee with Vivian.

"I apologize for the effect this unfortunate situation has had on you. Once I return to London and speak to the inspectors and visit the banks, and once those responsible are found and apprehended, you may return to your active social schedule."

The woman looked to him without warmth. It was as if Vivian watched two mere acquaintances. Then again, most people would find the fact a man's life was threatened distressful. How different this relationship was from his with the duchess.

"Well, I suppose it is only a week," she replied, then brightened. "I hope there will be many guests tonight. Perhaps I will hold a holiday fête at Woodhall."

"You can cohost with me for Twelfth Night," Duchess Torrington said, walking in.

Lady Yarnsby wrinkled her nose. "Perhaps."

Vivian and the duchess exchanged looks. "Claudia, we should adjourn to the parlor. Alexander is about to ask for Vivian's hand. We will be celebrating."

At the words, Lady Yarnsby stood. She looked around. "Where is Doxie?"

"Your little dog is in the parlor," Duchess Torrington replied.

Lady Yarnsby took Alexander's arm and practically dragged him out of the room.

Duchess Torrington shook her head. "You will not see her often. Claudia prefers superficial friends to a relationship with Alexander. Some women are like her; they cannot help the lack of maternal emotions."

"I do not understand it, Duchess Torrington, I really

do not."

"Call me Theresa, please. You are about to marry a man I consider a son."

Vivian nodded, unable to do so just yet. She still couldn't believe what was happening was real.

VIVIAN'S HEAD SWAM from all the activities of the evening. Toasts and good cheer ended the evening with everyone celebrating the arrival of a New Year. She'd barely had an opportunity to speak to Alexander as all his time was monopolized by his rather indulged mother.

As horrible as it was to think about, she was glad that Lady Yarnsby would be keeping her distance. It was obvious everyone tolerated her for Alexander's sake. The woman was insufferable. Just when Vivian thought to have found common ground upon learning Lady Yarnsby enjoyed helping the needy, the woman exclaimed on how taxing it was to send people out to do the work.

By the time everyone went to bed, Vivian was utterly exhausted.

She rolled to her side and looked at the door. Alexander slept just two doors down. It was possible to slip there unnoticed and have a word with him. They'd not had a chance to speak alone before he'd approached her father to ask for hand. Her wonderful, darling father, who'd asked her if she was in agreement before granting his blessing. Vivian had cried in that moment upon realizing that once she and Alexander married, she'd no longer have his company in the evenings.

Although his research of social matters was interesting, the depths to which her father delved were at times overwhelming. Despite being bored to tears, she did it because helping him sort through articles was time they spent alone together.

Slipping from the bed, Vivian pulled her robe on and tiptoed to the door. Once in the hallway, it would be impossible to hear anyone approaching as her heart hammered so hard, it echoed in her ears.

"Crumpets," she hissed when her toe slammed into a table in the hallway. Thankfully, she was able to grab the vase atop it before it crashed to the ground.

Limping the next few steps, she arrived at Alexander's door and lifted her hand to rap on it. Soft murmurs permeated through her heart's hammering.

"Oh no." Vivian opened Alexander's door and ducked inside just as Clara's voice became clearer.

Her sister and husband walked past, talking in hushed tones. If they were still up, then perhaps Alexander was too. "Goodness." Vivian blinked, willing her eyes to adjust to the darkness. Finally, she gave up.

"Alexander," she whispered. "Are you in here?"

Her hip hit something, and she reached out to ensure she knock something over. "God's foot, why is it so dark in here?"

"I like it dark," Alexander replied. "Stay there before you alert the entire household. I'm surprised your crash in the corridor didn't already."

Vivian gasped. "You heard that?"

It sounded as if he got out of the bed, then his warm hands took her arms. "Come sit, I will light a—"

"No, don't," Vivian said. "I look a fright, and besides, it could alert someone."

"You prefer to talk in the dark?" His words were tinged with amusement. "How about I part the curtains a bit?"

"Very well, but I'm coming with you. I don't care for the dark."

His arm rounded her waist, and she was grateful for the darkness as she was sure her cheeks were bright red.

Reaching out with her right hand, Vivian touched what she assumed was a bedpost and stopped. "I will wait right here."

Moments later, soft moonlight gave just enough light to make him out. In only bottoms, he wore nothing from the waist up. Her eyes rounded; she'd not considered what he'd wear to bed.

"Why are you half undressed?"

He looked down as if realizing it for the first time. "Because I was too tired to find my night clothes and didn't wish to bother searching. Most of my clothes are in a trunk there." He motioned toward a dark corner.

"I see. Aren't you cold?" Vivian couldn't stop staring at him. He had a wide chest with just a smattering of hair across it. Her eyes glazed over as she trailed her gaze down the center of his chest to his flat stomach.

"The blankets kept me warm enough. I'd best find my robe," Alexander said, his lips curving. "Else my bride-to-be may swoon."

"I don't swoon."

"Do you feel weak in the knees?" he asked, moving closer. "Is your breathing becoming labored?"

Vivian swallowed and inhaled deeply, doing her best to keep from taking another breath. When he came even closer, she gave up. "It's all the activity...coming here...in the dark."

"I see." He was so close, it would take so very little effort to touch him. Her hand lifted, but she caught the treacherous thing and ordered it back down to her side.

"Why did you come to my bedroom?" Alexander asked. "Curiosity?"

"Of course not." Vivian managed to sound annoyed. "I wished to...speak."

His lips hovered over hers. "No interest in kissing or touching me at all?" Alexander's breath fanned over her face, making her eyelids fall.

Would it be foolish to allow herself this? He was to be her husband, after all. Every inch of her body urged her forward. To touch, feel, enjoy.

"We...er...I'd better go. I'd hoped to speak to you, but I see it is not possible."

When his warm fingers trailed down the side of her face and cupped her jaw, Vivian knew she'd not leave.

"Are you curious to know how compatible we are physically?" Alexander asked. "I believe I know the answer."

Her robe seemed to fall from her body to pool around her feet. Vivian was too enthralled in his caresses, the warmth of his mouth over hers, and the feel of his bare skin pressed her body.

Of their own accord, her arms wrapped around him, welcoming what was to come. Already it was so beautiful as feelings she'd never experienced before overwhelmed her senses.

"You are so beautiful," Alexander said.

"As are you," Vivian replied without hesitation.

He smiled down at her. "I am glad you think so."

Alexander hurried to the bed and yanked the bedding from it, then placed it in front of the fireplace. He added a log to the waning flames, and the fire sprung to life.

It was as if she floated when he lifted her into his arms and carried her to lay on the floor, then joined her.

The room spun, her senses overcome by what was to happen. Was she really going to allow things to go this far? Her thoughts silenced when his body pressed against her. It was a feeling like no other. He was warm, hard, solid. The heat of his breath fanned over her face just before he pressed a kiss against the base of her throat.

A moan escaped when his hand slid up her leg, his fingers trailing lazily atop her skin as he licked wicked patters along her neck.

Suddenly it was overwhelming, the heat of the fire and her body combating with one another.

"Alexander," Vivian gasped. "I came to speak to you."

"About?" he asked against her ear. His breath sent tingles of awareness down her body. Meanwhile, his hand continued caressing her leg, moving up until reaching her hip.

"I-I can't think straight," she replied, grateful when he covered her mouth with his.

Vivian turned sideways, pressing against him, kissing him back hungrily.

He rolled onto his back, bringing her against his chest. "We should stop, else I may not be able to." His breathless words along with the lifting and lowering of his chest made Vivian giddy with the effect she had on him.

He pressed a kiss to her forehead. "Now tell me, what did you wish to speak about?"

CHAPTER ELEVEN

January 1818, London

"THEY WILL SHOW up," William said, his gaze pinning Alexander. "It is the right thing to do. You have to make a stand."

Along with the local constable and two inspectors, he and Alexander waited in the banker's office. The poor man looked about to faint, his face glossing with perspiration. Just as the man mopped his face, the pair they for waited for entered the bank.

A woman greeted them. Unlike the banker, she was not nervous as she'd not been appraised of what occurred.

"We are here to close an account," Bettina said, a handkerchief at the ready. "It is imperative that we meet with the banker."

"Who should I say is here?" the woman asked them.

Jasper and Bettina exchanged looked. Jasper cleared his throat. "Jasper and Bettina Yarnsby."

"Yarnsby?" Alex said and huffed.

William shrugged. "Helps them get in the door."

"Go out to them and ask what they need," the inspector prodded the banker, who once again mopped his face.

Somehow the banker managed to walk in a straight line. Everyone in the room strained to hear what happened next.

"I am Mr. Walters," the man said and hesitated. "How can I help you?" In the silence that followed, Alex assumed he was inviting them to sit at the newly positioned desk just outside the door where they all were.

"Unfortunately, our half-brother died recently," Bettina said with a loud sniff.

"His name was Alexander Yarnsby," Jasper added. "We are here to liquidate his account according to his wishes."

At the next moment of silence, the sound of papers being shuffled meant they brought paperwork to present.

"It is a rather large amount. You may have to return in a day or two," the banker replied after a few minutes.

"We can wait," Jasper said. "Can you tell me how much is available today?"

"I will check. If you would please give me a moment." The sound of a chair scraping meant the banker stood.

"Are you unwell?" Bettina asked. "You look about to faint."

"I've been suffering from upset stomach," the banker replied. "May I inquire how the young Mr. Yarnsby met his demise?"

"He fell ill," Bettina replied and sniffed. "It was very quick."

"My sincerest condolences," the banker replied. Footsteps neared, and the man entered the room. He let out a long breath and sunk into a chair.

Alexander gave the man an annoyed look. It wasn't as if

his life was threatened. He supposed knowing they'd attempted to kill him could be distressing.

"Mr. Yarnsby." The constable motioned for Alex to follow him out. "I will approach first to ensure they are not armed."

He bit back a curse and nodded. Following the man out, he kept his gaze sharp, needing to see the duo's reaction.

At first, they focused on the constable, then upon his appearance, their eyes widened.

Jasper jumped to his feet, his face contorted in rage. "Why aren't you dead?"

"You killed the wrong man," Alexander replied dryly.

Unlike her brother, Bettina seemed to shrink into the chair, her pale face turning white. She looked from Alex to her brother. "You said he was dead. How is this possible?"

"Shut up, Bettina," Jasper snapped. "Don't say a word."

Bettina began to sob, her thin shoulders shaking. "I don't want to be jailed." When she flailed and flopped onto the floor, Jasper took advantage of the distraction and sprinted to the front door.

Thankfully, the constable had posted two officers at the door, and he was nabbed immediately.

Jasper glared at Alexander. "Why should you get everything? He was our father; he should have left us something."

Despite the anger, Alex walked up to Jasper. "I allowed you to close one account and keep the money. Instead of taking that and quitting, you decide to kill me and take everything."

As there was nothing he could say in response, Jasper looked past him to his sister. "Bettina had nothing to do with this."

"We were informed by the local constable that you were both in Berkhamsted," the constable replied. "It will be up to the judge to decide your fates."

When Jasper was taken out, two other men escorted a still sobbing Bettina out. She looked at Alexander. "Father would not stand for any of this."

"If he was your father, he would have left you something," Alexander replied. "My father would not have left you without financial recourse."

Her face contorted with fury. "He was my father. He was."

Alexander remained rooted to the spot until William came up to him. "Let's review the papers they brought. Perhaps some of them are legitimate."

IT WAS LATE in the evening when Alexander finally put down the paper he'd read several times. An expert had arrived and authenticated only a birth certificate. Everything else was forged. The death certificate for Alexander, of course, as well as a copy of Lord Torrington's Last Will and Testament were fake. Both had William Torrington listed as their father. The mother was a woman named Natalia d'Arques.

"Now we know what N.D. stands for," William said in a flat tone.

"What now?" Alexander asked the inspector who'd remained at the bank with them.

He'd met the man only once before and admired his dedication to maintaining law and order in London. The man stroked his mustache. "We will be in touch with you once we question them. All the evidence must be reviewed."

"Thank you," Alex replied, watching the papers being placed into an attaché.

THE TOWNHOUSE WAS silent as they entered. After so much activity at Lark's Song, the stillness of the townhouse stood out.

George, the butler, walked into the parlor with them. "Your correspondence," he said, holding out a tray with several envelopes.

Alexander looked at him. "For me or William?"

"For you. Obviously, news has reached the ears of eager hostesses that you are in town." The man's dry tone made him bite back a chuckle.

William laughed. "I wonder how many you would have received if they'd been aware you are to be married?"

As Alexander leafed through the invitations, he discounted one after another. "One." He held up an invitation for dinner from Lord and Lady Barrow.

He placed the invitation down and sat. "It is as if instead of a burden being lifted, a heavier one is on my shoulders now," Alex said. "It seems they are my father's children."

"They should have gone about things legally. Instead, they allowed resentment to misguide them." William handed him a glass of brandy. "Alex, look at me."

When Alex met the eyes of the man he considered to be his only brother, there was strength.

"Alex, you could have been dead. Believe me when I tell you this—if they'd succeeded, I would have ensured their demise."

His eyes widened at the truth of William's words. "They would not have lived past arriving at the bank. Instead of the constable, I would have had others with me that would not be as…law abiding."

Finally, Alexander nodded, acknowledging that it was out of his hands now. "I will ask to speak to them, then make a decision about whether or not to speak on their behalf. I have a feeling it is not Jasper who was behind the entire thing. He spoke up, but did you notice how he kept looking to her? As if for approval."

"I did."

HE'D NEVER BEEN in a jail cell before, and Alexander hoped to never have to be in one again. Jasper sat inside, his head hanging, not willing to look at him.

"Jasper," Alex started. "Do you wish to know who the man you killed was?"

Jasper's head came up. "No. It is best that I don't know."

"He is the reason you may die here."

Closing his eyes, Jasper took a shaky breath. "How did things go this far?"

"Where is your mother?"

At the change of subject, the man finally looked to him. "In France. I'd gone there as well, to live."

"But Bettina came for you. She convinced you to return to England, didn't she?"

Instead of a response, Jasper took another shaky breath. "It is like I said, I was the one who did everything. It was all my plan."

"What kind of poison did you use?"

Jasper frowned. "Rat poison."

"Is wasn't," Alex said flatly, noting Jasper stiffened. "What did you put the poison in?"

"The tea…" Jasper gave up. He had no idea. "I hired someone to do it, so I am not sure."

"A man there to repair the roof saw a woman leaving the house one morning." Alex hesitated. "Slender and pale with dark hair."

Jasper shook his head. "It is not possible."

"Admit it. Bettina is the one who was not satisfied with the amount you stole from one account. I know this because she is the one who went to the forger, not you."

Jasper met his gaze. "I will not speak against my sister. She only wanted to claim what is rightfully ours. Don't you understand? Our entire lives, you lived like a prince while we got whatever our father decided to give Mother."

"I was sent away to boarding school. I was raised by another family," Alex said, staring at him, daring him to look away. "I have seen Father's ledgers. The monthly stipend Father gave your mother is staggering. Enough to live at the same level as my own mother. You should have checked everything before going on this desperate journey. Your mother lied to both you and your sister."

Jasper's expression changed. Upon arriving in France, he must have been shocked at his mother's living situation. No doubt the woman lived well on the money she'd been keeping for herself.

"It looks as though our father preferred selfish, distant women," Alex said. "I'm sorry."

"Bettina...she is not a good person, but she's my only sister, and I care deeply for her."

Alex studied Jasper. There was a bit of resemblance to his father in the shape of his nose and lips; the dark eye color and pale skin he must have gotten from his mother. It was a striking combination. "I regret to get to know you under these circumstances."

His half-brother shook his head. "Bettina is not Father's daughter. She was already born when Mother and he met. I think she's always felt left out because of it. Although he was generous in his affections toward me, he often ignored her."

There was so much to say, but at the same time not enough. Alex realized that Jasper was young and impressionable. "How old are you?"

"Eighteen."

"I will speak to the judge on your behalf. However, I doubt there is little that can be done for Bettina. She killed a man."

CHAPTER TWELVE

V IVIAN KEPT VIGIL from the dining room table, where everyone had eaten and one by one, meandered away.

Ladies Torrington and Yarnsby, along with her mother, had gone to the Torringtons home to prepare for the Twelfth Night celebration. The duke and her father had gone as well. It was gratifying to see that all the parents got along so well.

Clara and Penelope had gone for a ride to the village, and although they'd insisted she go with them, Vivian wished for some quiet time alone.

"Would you like to go for a walk?" Mary, her wonderful companion, neared and lowered to a chair. "It will make the wait better."

She reached for Mary's hand and squeezed it. "You're right. But I find that I am enjoying the quiet of this moment. How do you feel about moving here with me, Mary?" Vivian had been avoiding asking. The idea of Mary leaving her side saddened her greatly.

Mary looked out the window, her face a study in calmness. "I like this place. It gives me peace. I will not mind it at all."

Letting out a long breath, Vivian smiled widely. "I was scared to ask you. If you would have preferred to remain in London, it would have broken my heart. Mother would have insisted you remain at the house, so you should not worry about not having employment."

"I prefer to come here," Mary said with a soft smile. "It is not so far from London that I cannot see my parents on occasion." She then added, "I wish to remain with you."

Mary's mother was Jamaican and her father British. They were kind people who Vivian had visited with Mary quite a few times.

"They will be welcome to come visit as often as they wish, you know that."

"Mother will enjoy it so very much. She loves getting away from London on occasion. Someone arrives," Mary said and stood. "It may be Mr. Yarnsby."

It was indeed Alexander who entered and went to her directly. He pulled Vivian into a tight hug. It was most unusual for a man to openly show affection, but Vivian loved it.

Vivian melted against him, reassured to know he returned unharmed. "I was afraid something horrible would happen to you." She lifted her face to him and was rewarded with a soft kiss.

"I will tell you about it. First, allow me to hold you a bit longer." The hoarseness in his voice made Vivian wonder what had happened, but she refrained from asking and allowed the embrace to linger.

The thought of Alexander becoming a constant in her life brought tingles of excitement. She couldn't wait to know what it would be like to be fully his. To experience the magic of lovemaking again. Although the night she'd sneaked to his bedchamber, they'd not gone so far as him claiming her virginity, she'd learned enough to know that when it happened, he would not disappoint.

"I cannot wait to live with you and spend every day together," Vivian said. "I know we will be very happy, Alexander."

He took a deep breath and slowly released her. When he met her gaze, there was warmth in his. "I missed you. It will be very hard to be away from you until our wedding. Tell me we will not prolong it."

Vivian bit her bottom lip. "I have an idea."

His brow furrowed. "I am afraid to ask."

"Did you not like the intimacy and lack of pomp of Clara and William's wedding?"

He nodded, and his lips curved.

Twelfth Night at Haven Estate

THE HOUSE WAS alit with candles, and there were many more people than Vivian had expected. When she and Penelope entered, Vivian gasped at the beautiful décor in the parlor.

"It's exactly as I wished it," she exclaimed. "Do you not think it perfect?"

Penelope gave her a curious look, then nodded. "It is."

Everyone important in her life was there. Alexander, her family, the Torringtons, Lady Yarnsby, and the

Barrows, who'd arrived the night before.

Music wafted through the house as Vivian made her way to find her mother. Just as she passed a mirror, she paused at noticing her own bright expression. Mary had styled her hair with the top brought up and pinned, and the back of her hair flowed down past her shoulders in carefully formed curls. She wore a green gown with soft white ruffles down the sides of the skirt. The round neckline was modest but flattering.

"You look radiant," her mother exclaimed at seeing her. "I knew that gown would be flattering, but my darling, you are stunning."

"I must speak to you," Vivian said, pulling her into a room that turned out to be a library. "Mother, I plan to…"

There was a light knock at the door, and Duchess Torrington peered in. "Lord and Lady Barrow have a surprise for us."

Everyone gathered in the parlor. Penelope leaned into Vivian's ear. "Where is Alexander?"

She'd been so intent on finding her mother, she'd not noticed he was missing. "I don't know. I'm sure he will be here shortly."

Lord Barrow cleared his throat and looked to Lady Barrow, who beamed. "I am so pleased that those closest to us will help welcome our son home."

At Gideon Barrow's entering, Clara, Penelope, and Vivian rushed to him. They'd grown up knowing each other and hated every long year he'd been gone after being sent away.

He'd left a young, easygoing man and returned a handsome, somewhat brooding man. His gaze was familiar, but it was hard to recognize the Gideon she'd known. His jaw was harder, his cheekbones sharper.

"Has he always had such long eyelashes?" Penelope whispered. "My goodness, he has changed."

Vivian chuckled. "Having second thoughts about marrying Tommy?"

"Of course not," Penelope snapped, making her laugh.

After everyone took turns speaking to Gideon, he promised to tell them about his adventures the next day. "This night, after all, is about celebrating the holiday," he told them.

"I have a surprise as well," William said, getting everyone's attention.

Vivian frowned. If everyone was going to have surprises, hers would end up being a disappointment, if she got to share it at all. By the way things were going, dinner would be served at any moment, and there would not be a chance for her surprise.

"Vivian." Clara took her arm. "Come with me. Hurry."

Her stomach sunk. Where was Alexander? Perhaps he'd changed his mind and would not marry her after all. "What is it? Tell me without hesitation. It's bad, isn't it?"

"Don't be silly. This was your idea." Clara tugged her. "Please move faster."

When they walked past an arched doorway, they entered a dome-covered courtyard. In the center was an elevated arbor. It was there Alexander stood with a clergyman.

He hurried down the steps, put his hands at her waist, and lifted her for a kiss. "Surprise, my love."

"I can't cry," Vivian exclaimed. "It will ruin everything." She managed a wobbly smile.

"Join us." He held her hand and led her up the steps to stand before the cleric as everyone burst out into the atrium. There were exclamations and applause.

Vivian looked to her mother and Duchess Torrington, and both had smug expressions of having known all along.

She turned to Alexander. "How long have you been planning this? I thought it was my idea."

"Since the day after I proposed. It is actually my aunt and your mother's plan. They suspected we'd not wait long to be intimate."

Her eyes widened, and she looked to the clergyman. Thankfully, he was too busy looking around the room at everyone who was trying their best to get settled.

"This is so wonderful," Vivian said with a sniff.

"Dearly Beloved…" The clergyman began, and everyone settled to witness the exchange of vows.

Vivian heard very little. In the moment, she was lost, her every thought on the fact that she was to be Alexander Yarnsby's wife. Repeating the vows took concentration as her entire being hummed with anticipation of what was to come—a lifetime of happy moments like these surrounded by the most wonderful group of people in her life.

"Thank you," she said, looking to the group after she and Alexander were pronounced husband and wife. "I am so very lucky to have each and every one of you in my life."

Even Lady Yarnsby, who wiped her eyes, showed emotion. Vivian smiled warmly at Mary, who stood with Penelope and Clara's companion, Molly.

It was the most perfect of days.

CHAPTER THIRTEEN

"I WONDERED WHERE we would spend our wedding night. I didn't expect it to be here," Vivian said, her voice trembling.

They were still at Haven in a large bedchamber that was decorated beautifully. The air was perfumed since there were several vases spilling over with beautiful greenery and red berries that must have taken hours to find.

Her hand trembled as she pulled pins from her hair, unsure exactly what to do after. Should she brush it out and change in front of Alexander?

Sure, he'd already seen her in her nightclothes, but this was to be so very different. The last time they'd been alone. They'd talked for hours, then he'd helped her into her robe and ensured she returned to her own bedroom without being seen.

"You think too much." Alexander pressed a kiss to her shoulder. "Turn around."

Vivian did as told, trembling when his fingers touched her skin as he unbuttoned the dress and slipped it from her shoulders.

He removed the next layer, his gaze holding hers in the mirror the entire time. Vivian could barely breathe as more and more of her body was exposed.

When she stood in only her stockings, he rolled them down, deftly pulling them and her slippers off.

"Vivian?"

She looked at his face. His warm gaze met hers for a moment before moving down the length of her body.

For some reason, the way he seemed to appreciate what he saw emboldened her, and Vivian was not embarrassed.

She moved closer to him and undid his cravat, followed by his vest. When she fumbled with the jacket, he yanked it off and tossed it. Soon after, he stood bare from the waist up.

They crashed into each other, his mouth claiming hers like a prize that was offered freely. Vivian wrapped her arms around his shoulders and shook with anticipation.

As if needing to ensure she was there, his hands traveled from her upper back, down to cup her bottom, then up her sides. Every place he touched felt like she was being branded as his and his alone.

Vivian wanted more, needed to be overtaken. If only she wasn't so untrained in what to do. Perhaps she should have read Penelope's lovemaking book. She raked her fingers down his back to his waist.

When his mouth pressed on the side of her neck, she allowed it to fall sideways, her eyes closing.

Alexander lifted her easily into his arms, then carried her to the bed, lowering her gently. The cool bedding sent awareness of what was to happen through her, and Vivian sat up.

What a reward it was to see Alexander finish undressing. His body was like a work of art. Every part of him was so very different than her own. His chest was wide with a sprinkling of hair, his arms well formed. There were ripples that went from under his ribs to a flat stomach. Between his legs, just below a patch of hair, was something she'd never seen before.

Vivian could not pull her eyes away from his arousal. It was as she'd often heard said, the male species had an appendage to use to mount the female species.

As much as she'd tried to picture what they had, she'd not dreamed of what she saw now.

Her hand itched to touch and feel it.

"May I touch you?" Her voice sounded hoarse as her mouth had turned dry.

Alexander nodded and walked closer.

Meeting his gaze, she felt her cheeks warm. "Will it hurt if I press on it?"

"It is like any other part of my body. A bit sensitive right now as I am aroused."

At first, she was tentative, sliding two fingers from the base to the tip. Alexander watched her with curiosity but said nothing.

When Vivian wrapped her hand around it, his sharp intake of breath made her draw her hand away. "I am sorry."

"It did not hurt," he said in a strained voice. "It excites me when you do that."

"Oh," Vivian replied, studying him and then his staff.

"It is soft to the touch and yet hard."

Alexander lowered to the bed, and she was disappointed as she'd hope to explore his sex more.

When he pulled her closer, his mouth taking hers, Vivian forgot about the curiosity that was soon replaced with ardor.

"Breathe," Alexander instructed between kisses when his fingers slid down the center of her legs. Each touch made her jump at the unusual sensations.

"Relax. Close your eyes," he told her next when she pushed his hand away. "Enjoy it, Vivian."

Forcing herself to do as he said, Vivian let out a breath and waited. The warmth of his kisses felt wonderful as he trailed his mouth down from her neck to take first one breast tip into his mouth, then the other.

When she began to wiggle as heat pooled between her legs, Alexander once again touched her. This time his fingers circled her core, each caress spreading heat down her legs.

Vivian gasped and her breathing became jagged whenever the sensations threatened to overtake and send her reeling.

Finally, when she could not stand it any longer, he came over her. She searched his face for answers as to what he'd do next, but he looked down between them.

Taking himself in hand, Alexander guided his staff to her entrance.

She tensed, waiting for him to impale her, but instead, he did what he'd done with his fingers and slid it up and down her sex. The sensation was absolutely wonderful, and soon, Vivian was lost.

A sharp pain cut through her excitement, and she cried out.

"What did you do?" she said, pushing at his shoulders. "It hurt."

"Shh." Alexander kissed her face. "It will lessen, I promise."

It did. He began to move, immediately sending all thoughts of pain away.

Lovemaking was like nothing Vivian could have ever conjured up on her own. If his kisses had made her knees weak, his caresses sent her to swoon, and this, the joining, made her fly.

Vivian begged him not to stop moving as it was so utterly wonderful. Indescribable sensations that she would never be able to explain assaulted her, one after another.

Through the haze of movements, touching and kissing, Alexander's masculine grunts permeated, making it even more enjoyable.

Suddenly there was a change, and her body became uncontrollable. Vivian fought to keep herself from it, but then it was as if she were a crystal that broke into millions of pieces.

LANGUID AND UNABLE to move, Vivian was sprawled over her husband. She'd demanded the repeat lovemaking again, and now it was almost dawn.

Both were too spent to do more than lay in a pool of

bedding.

"I think we will not make breakfast this morning," he said groggily.

Vivian's lips curved. "We may not make midday tea either."

His deep chuckles made her stomach do funny things, and she let out a sigh.

"I love you, Alexander Yarnsby."

He lifted his head and hitched an eyebrow. "I hope so, Mrs. Yarnsby, since you have thoroughly seduced me."

EPILOGUE

Spring 1818, Berkhamsted

"**Y**OU ABSOLUTELY MUST come for at least a month," Penelope demanded. Draped across a settee in the sitting room of the huge Yarnsby home, she looked every bit a damsel in distress.

Her sister had been doing her best to convince both her and Clara to come to London to attend the balls.

"Clara's title will do much more for you this season that I could ever hope for," Vivian replied indulgently. "Even though Alexander has a title, he still refuses to use it."

"What about when you have children? Won't your first son have a right to it?" Penelope straightened when Mary entered with a tray. "Mary will you please convince my sister that it is imperative she come to London for my coming out."

Vivian could not stand it any longer. "Very well. If you do not stop clamoring, my head will split in two."

Although it was early morning, the day was already sunny. The duchess would arrive soon, and they planned to go birdwatching. It was exciting as they'd never ventured out in the area around Alexander's family home. Later that day, once Clara and William arrived, a picnic was planned on the grounds.

"Married life suits you," Penelope announced. "You're glowing with happiness. I'm going to look like you when I marry Tommy."

Unable to keep from it, Vivian let out a happy sigh. "I am so very happy." She studied her sister for a moment. "Have you seen Gideon since his return?"

"He rarely leaves home. Lady Barrow says she is afraid he may have some sort of ill-affect after being away at war for so long."

"Poor dear," Vivian said. "You should make an effort. Go visit him."

Penelope sat up and shook her head. "I tried and he practically threw me out. I am not going to put myself out to be mistreated. I promised Lady Barrow to attempt again. Perhaps I will bring a stick and beat him with it, if he acts the same."

"He did seem changed," Vivian replied. "If anyone can get someone out of their shell however, it is you dear sister. It is a challenge you will definitely fight and win."

"Of course, I will win," Penelope said. "I never lose a fight."

TWO DAYS LATER, they traveled to Lark's Song, where they

were to spend the next week. Alexander insisted it would be easier for everyone to gather if closer to the Duke and Duchess. Vivian had to agree. As much as she loved the huge estate where she now lived, it was much too far from everyone.

Alexander had left the day before along with, Clara and the others. Vivian considered that she'd noticed Alexander being extra secretive the last few days.

"Mary?" she asked her companion. "Have you heard anything from Harold about my husband's latest project? He and William have meet with an army of men as of late. He insists it has to do with building the larger stables, but they have never gone out and walked around the grounds."

Her companion shook her head. "I can ask Thomas," she said referring to the coachman, who Mary was sweet on. Thomas had already declared himself, they were just waiting on their parents to arrive to make is formal.

Vivian looked forward to entertaining both Thomas' and Mary's parents. She'd insisted rooms be prepared for them on the bottom floor. There were enough for an army of servants.

Upon nearing Lark's Song, Thomas rode past the normal turn, and continued down a narrow road.

"Where are we going?" Vivian asked.

Mary stuck her head out the window and called out to Thomas, asking the same question. She ducked back in. "He said to be following Mr. Alexander's instructions."

"Oh, a surprise," Penelope exclaimed with a bright smile. "I do adore surprises."

Vivian frowned. "I am not sure I share your enthusiasm

for them. If anything, it makes me feel anxious. What if something is wrong? Or if I do not like whatever it is? Do I have to feign to be excited?"

"You make too much of it," Penelope said. "Sit back and enjoy the moment."

It was just a few minutes later when the carriage came to a stop. She looked out, and other than there being some sort of wall structure, Vivian could not see anything else, in the large empty field.

Alexander came to the door and opened it. "If you will excuse us ladies," he said looking to Penelope and Mary. "I must speak to my wife."

Heart hammering and stomach in jumbles, she allowed her husband to help her from the carriage. "What is it Alexander?" She looked around noting that four men were lined up beside the half-erected structure.

"I wanted to wait to share this with you, but the more they build, the more you would be able to see it, when we visit Lark's Song."

"What exactly are they building?" Vivian said giving the men a puzzled look.

Alexander frowned. "I hope you will be glad. My uncle, the duke, he clarified needlessly, gave me a large plot of land. I offered to purchase it, but he claims it was already in my name."

When he paused, Vivian still did not understand. "Alex, pray tell me what you are doing."

His lips curved and he motioned to the men and the structure. "Darling, I am having a home built for us here. Closer to our family."

With a squeal of happiness, Vivian did the most uncharacteristic thing and jumped up into Alexander's arms, wrapping her arms around his neck. He laughed and twirled in a circle.

"I can scarcely believe it. We will be able to visit with Clara and William all the time." She smiled so wide, her cheeks ached.

"You are happy then?" Alexander asked kissing her soundly.

She didn't care that the men looked on or that Penelope and Mary came running at hearing her scream.

The next story in this series is Mary Asher's story, Vivian's companion. When Mary meets the handsome Irish coachman, sparks fly. *The Allure of a Reformed Rogue* is part of an anthology.

A SHORT EXCERPT –
THE ALLURE OF A REFORMED ROGUE

MARY TOOK A spoonful of porridge and ate it. It was hard to keep from stealing a glance at the quiet man across the table from her. She peered up, pretending interest in the window behind him.

His shorn, light brown hair had just a hint of auburn, the same for his eyebrows. There was a shadow of a beard on his jaw, which looked to be a shade darker. His eye color seemed to change between green and blue, she supposed they were hazel if one were to describe them.

Taller than her by half a foot, he had the masculine build of a man whose work required physical effort. She would not describe him as astonishingly fetching, but he was handsome in an understated way. If asked, she would call him attractive. Yes, that was it. Thomas Sullivan was very attractive.

"Excuse me?" He studied her. "Who do you refer to?"

Her eyes widened. The annoying habit of mumbling when she thought often got her into difficult situations. "Err… I was thinking that Lottie is right. Mr. Yarnsby and Miss Vivian make an attractive couple."

Thankfully, Moira interjected. "Oh, they do, and so well suited."

"Indeed," Lottie, who'd yet to get up, added.

Thomas ate the rest of his breakfast in silence and then stood, put his bowl on the counter, and walked out. It was as if he'd rather be anywhere but around people.

"Do you think he is shy or just does not care for our company?" Mary asked, looking toward the now closed door. "Certainly, seems in a hurry to leave our company every morning."

"Rarely asks for a second serving," Moira said. "He does linger at times."

Lottie huffed. "Only when you are here alone, Moira. He must dislike either me or Mary."

"It does not matter," Mary said, standing. "I best see about preparing for the day. First I will inspect the garden."

Wrapping her shawl around her shoulders, she went out to look over the garden area. It was only ten days that she'd come to live at Woodhall, and the size of the huge home still astonished her. Upon turning to the back of the house, where the garden was, she stopped in her tracks, finding Thomas.

He stood with his head bent and hands clasped against his chest, as if in prayer. Like most Irish, he was probably a devout Catholic. Mary turned to leave just as Moira's huge orange cat made its way to the kitchen for its morning bowl of milk.

Despite her attempt to avoid the animal, the cat weaved around her legs. Mary did her best to walk away to avoid being seen by Thomas and unfortunately lost her balance when the cat continued its pattern around her ankles.

She fell to the ground on all fours. "Crumpets, George," she hissed at the cat, who sat at the doorstep and glared at her. "Bad kitty." While Mary scrambled to stand, the wind blew her shawl over her head, so she couldn't see.

"I will help you up." Thomas took her left arm and pulled her up to stand.

About the Author

Enticing. Engaging. Romance.

USA Today Bestselling Author Hildie McQueen writes Medieval Scottish Romance, Regency, and American Historical Romance. If you like stories with a mixture of passion, drama and humor, you will love Hildie's storytelling. Strong alpha heroes meet their match and fall in love every time in Hildie's books.

Hildie's favorite pastimes are reader conventions, traveling, shopping and reading.

A fan of all things pink, Paris, and four legged creatures, Hildie resides in eastern Georgia, USA, with her super-hero husband Kurt and four little yappy dogs.